THE CAT WHO...
QUIZ BOOK

Most Berkley Books are available at special quantity discounts for bulk purchases for sales promotions, premiums, fund-raising, or educational use. Special books, or book excerpts, can also be created to fit specific needs.

For details, write: Special Markets, The Berkley Publishing Group, 375 Hudson Street, New York, New York 10014.

The Cat Who....
Quiz Book

M HEADRIC 2003

ROBERT J. HEADRICK, JR.

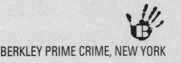
BERKLEY PRIME CRIME, NEW YORK

A Berkley Prime Crime Book
Published by The Berkley Publishing Group
A division of Penguin Group (USA) Inc.
375 Hudson Street
New York, New York 10014

This book is an original publication of The Berkley Publishing Group.

THE CAT WHO . . . QUIZ BOOK

PRINTING HISTORY
Berkley Prime Crime trade paperback edition / November 2003

Berkley Prime Crime trade paperback ISBN: 0-425-19187-7

This title has been registered with the Library of Congress.

PRINTED IN THE UNITED STATES OF AMERICA

10 9 8 7 6 5 4 3 2 1

ACKNOWLEDGMENTS

First, thanks to my mom and dad for their constant support and encouragement in all things that I do. Thanks also to my sister, Beth; her husband, Chuck; my nieces, Haley (and her husband, Tom) and Hilary; and my nephew, Aaron.

Thanks also to Martha Williams, Nashville, Tennessee, who first introduced me to *The Cat Who . . .* series. Thanks also to Kathleen White, Wellsboro, Pennsylvania, for her comments on the format and types of questions I ask about each book in the series.

Thanks to all the wonderful people in Moose County, who share their lives with us. Thanks also to Lilian Jackson Braun, "The Lady Who . . ." created these characters and enables us to step out of our own lives and into the lives of Qwill, Koko, and Yum Yum. Thanks also to Ms. Braun for believing there should be a quiz book to accompany the series.

Thanks to Sharon A. Feaster who gave us the definitive sourcebook, *The Cat Who . . . Companion*, which enables us to better acquaint ourselves with all things "Cat Who . . ." Her book was a constant "companion" to me as I wrote questions and created sections around which to structure the quizzes. Thanks also to Julie Murphy and Sally Abney Stempinski, who in their companion volume to the series, *The Cat Who . . . Cookbook*, provide recipes for many of the inspired menus enjoyed by Qwill and his friends.

Thanks to Natalee Rosenstein, whose call inviting me to proceed with this project was a welcome one. Also thanks to her assistant, Esther Strauss, who was quick to respond to my E-mails and requests and whose editorial expertise freed this book from many inconsistencies, redundancies, and in the end made it a much better book!

Thanks also to Abby Kreutz, technology specialist, who quickly and patiently responded to all of my loud screams when files disappeared for no apparent reasons! Thanks for managing to save all of my files!

Finally, thanks to Frank, who introduced me to Vandy, the first Scottish Fold "Cat Who . . ." and then later to our three "Cats Who . . .": Red, Cleo, and Toni. There was hardly a day that passed, while writing this book, that under my feet, on my desk, in an office chair, or on stacks of completed manuscript pages, one or all of the "Cats Who . . ." didn't manage to find a place to sit . . . as if, of course, to say they approved of the book. I suspect, too, they are equally glad to see that it's finally finished.

CONTENTS

FOREWORD

Lilian Jackson Braun

How will the good folk of Moose County respond to *The Cat Who . . . Quiz Book*?

Jim Qwilleran will huff into his moustache and write a thousand laudatory words for the "Qwill Pen" column.

Polly Duncan will quote Shakespeare: "*I am amazed and know not what to say.*"

Koko will sum it up in two well-chosen syllables: "Yow-wow!"

My compliments to Robert J. Headrick, Jr., on his bright idea, diligent research, and tantalizing questions!

I predict he has invented a new game that anyone can play, young or old—anyone, that is, who reads *The Cat Who* . . . chronicles. I predict there will be Pickax Parties throughout the English-speaking world: family discussions at the dinner table, long-distance phone calls between friends, contests among the Internet fan clubs, powwows in the coffee shops, and seminars in the public libraries. Participants will find satisfaction in demonstrating their eye for details and memory quotient.

Congratulations, Robert, on masterminding a stimulating challenge and entertaining adventure!

As Thelma Thackeray would say, if she were here, "I couldn't have done better myself, ducky!"

INTRODUCTION

I recall reading my first *The Cat Who . . .* mystery and thinking what an enjoyable experience it was! Like so many others, I was hooked. Since I began with *The Cat Who Talked to Ghosts*, it seemed wise to go back and start from the beginning. So I proceeded to go back to the beginning and start the series. From that point on, I couldn't wait to see what Qwill and the cats would do next. As I moved from one book to another in the series, I began to grow increasingly anxious about all of the people I was meeting and their relationships with each other and their marvelous qualities and characteristics. There were so many places and people to remember. And of course there was the food and the restaurants, and I continued to imagine what it would be like to move from one place to another like Qwill. How to remember it all? And just about that time, Sharon Feaster's *The Cat Who . . . Companion* book appeared. Finally, everything was organized for me so that as I continued to read books in the series and increase my understanding of the characters and their relationships in the series, I grew increasingly comfortable with each.

I guess it was the academic in me that caused me to think: *One day wouldn't it be fun to create a series of questions around each of the books in the series?* As a former teacher and college professor, I've spent so much of my time reading critically that I often find myself jotting comments or questions in the margins of books I am reading . . . not as much now as I used to, but I must confess I still do it. So I guess it was natural for me to gravitate to wanting to write a series of questions for each book. Is it really important that we remember the population of Pickax City or what Polly's father's name is or who ate what at which restaurant or what the layout is of each of Qwill's "gracious abodes"? Probably not, but it does nevertheless make for great conversation when you are talking with another fan of the series. Like me, I am sure you, too, discover new things about Qwill or Koko and Yum Yum or Polly each time you read a book or go back and read one again. Clues may have escaped you on the first reading. How many times have you gotten to the concluding chapters where everything is explained and said to yourself, "That's it!" or "Now it all adds up!"

The quizzes that accompany each book in the series are divided into several different parts, each testing the reader's recall of information related to such things as the women in Qwill's life, the food, the clues to the mystery, the houses in which he lives, and the behaviors exhibited by Koko and Yum Yum. There are also general questions that focus on specific details about the work in its entirety. And finally, there is a section in which the reader is asked to arrange a series of events from the story in chronological order.

I tried to balance the level of difficulty of the questions so that many can be answered after only a first reading of the book. But there will be some questions that will require a second, more careful reading. While some questions are very specific, I also tried to include a series of more general questions that would lead to a better understanding of the character development and interplay between characters obvious in many of the books.

Readers will also find a series of quizzes that are more comprehensive and cumulative. These quizzes appear at the end of every fifth book in the series and pull information about specific characters, places, clues, and Qwill from the preceding books. There are also several comprehensive quizzes about specific characters (those appearing most frequently in the series) as well as businesses and other topics of interest.

Readers will also be able to test their knowledge on the original short stories collected in *The Cat Who Had 14 Tales* and the more recent legends as told in Qwill's *Short & Tall Tales*.

I hope you enjoy *The Cat Who . . . Quiz Book* as you read and reread the exploits of Qwill and Koko and Yum Yum.

THE EASY ONES!

Here are some easy questions to get you started. The answers to each of these questions are probably right on the tip of your tongue! Good luck!

1. What is the name of the author of *The Cat Who* . . . series?

2. What is Qwill's full name?

3. What is the title of the first book in the series?

4. What is the title of the last book in the series (as of January 2003)?

5. In which book is the phrase "400 miles north of everywhere" first used?

6. In which book does Yum Yum join Qwill and Koko?

7. What is the population of Pickax?

8. Where exactly is Pickax City?

9. What is Moose County's new newspaper called?

10. What position does Polly hold at the Pickax Public Library?

11. What snack food does Celia Robinson make and send to the cats?

12. What is the name of the foundation started by Qwilleran?

13. What is the name of the department store in downtown Pickax?

14. What is the address of the Klingenschoen Mansion?

15. What is the name of the original Pickax newspaper?

16. Who are Bootsie (a.k.a. Bigfoot) and Brutus?

17. Qwill shortened Koko's name from what?

18. What is the name of the law firm that represents the Klingenschoen Foundation?

19. Which restaurant in Pickax has the "second worst coffee in Moose County?"

20. What river is often referred to in the series?

21. What is the name of the short story that launched the writing career of Ms. Braun?

22. Prior to her writing career, Ms. Braun worked for a metropolitan newspaper. Can you name it?

23. What is the slogan of the *Daily Fluxion*?

24. What is the name of the water Qwill drinks often?

25. What is the name of the book Qwill writes about legends of Moose County?

IN THE BEGINNING . . .

Beginnings play an important role in establishing the setting of each of *The Cat Who . . .* mysteries. Can you name the mystery based on the beginning?

1. "In late August, sixteen residents of Moose County, a remote part of the United States 400 miles north of everywhere, traveled to Scotland for a tour of the Western Isles and Highlands, lochs and moors, castles and crofts, firths and straths. . . . Only fifteen of them returned alive, and the survivors straggled home in various states of shock and confusion."

2. "It was a September to remember! In Moose County, 400 miles north of everywhere, plans were rife and hopes were high. First, the historic hotel of Pickax City, the county seat, was finally restored after the bombing of the previous year, and it would reopen with a new name, a new chef, and a gala reception. . . . Next, a distinguished personage from Chicago had reserved the presidential suite and would arrive on Labor Day, setting female hearts aflutter."

3. "A man of middle age, with a large, drooping moustache and brooding eyes, hunched over the steering wheel and gripped the rim anxiously as he maneuvered his car up a mountain road that was narrow, unpaved, and tortuous. Unaccustomed to mountain driving, he found it a blood-curdling ordeal."

4. "Following an unseasonable thaw and disastrous flooding, spring came early to Moose County, 400 miles north of everywhere. In Pickax City, the county seat, flowerboxes on Main Street were blooming in April, birds were singing in Park Circle, mosquitoes were hatching in the bogs, and strangers were beginning to appear in the campgrounds and on the streets of downtown."

5. "It was a strange winter in Moose County, 400 miles north of everywhere. First, there was disagreement about the long-range weather forecast. The weatherman at the local radio station predicted a winter of zero temperature, daily snow, minus-sixty windchill, and paralyzing blizzards—in other words: normal. . . . The weather was only the first strange happening of the winter, however. In December, an outbreak of petty larceny dampened the holiday spirit in Pickax. Trivial items began to disappear from cars and public places."

6. "World-shaking news was seldom broadcast by WPKX, the radio station serving Moose County, 400 miles north of everywhere. Local baseball scores, another car accident, a fire in a chicken coop and death notices were the usual fare. In late June, listeners snapped to attention, then, when a Sunday evening newspaper included this bulletin: 'An unidentified backpacker of no known address may or may not be a missing person, according to Moose County authorities. . . .'"

7. "The WPKX radio announcer hunched over the newsdesk in front of a dead microphone, anxiously fingering his script and waiting for the signal to go on the air. The station was filling in with classical music. The lilting 'Anitra's Dance' seemed hardly appropriate under the circumstances. Abruptly the music stopped in the middle of a bar, and the newscaster began to read in a crisp, professional tone that belied the alarming nature of the news: 'We interrupt this program to bring you a bulletin on the forest fires that are rapidly approaching Moose County after destroying hundreds of square miles to the south and the west. . . .'"

8. "Jim Qwilleran, whose name had confounded typesetters and proofreaders for two decades, arrived fifteen minutes early for his appointment with the managing editor of the *Daily Fluxion*. . . . He read the weather prediction (unseasonably warm) and the circulation figures (427,463) and the publisher's slogan. . . ."

9. "Autumn, in that year of surprises, was particulary delicious in Moose County, 400 miles north of everywhere. Not only had most of the summer vacationers gone home, but civic-awareness groups and enthusiastic *foodies* were cooking up a savory kettle of stew called the Great Food Explo. . . ."

10. "September promised to be a quiet month in Moose County, that summer vacation paradise 400 miles north of everywhere. After Labor Day the tourists returned to urban turmoil in the cities Down Below; the black fly season ended; children went reluctantly back to school; and everyday life cranked down to its normal, sleepy pace. This year the siesta was short-lived, however. Within a week the community was jolted by news of the Orchard Incident, as it was headlined by the local newspaper. . . ."

11. "The news that reached Pickax City early on that cold November morning sent a deathly chill through the small northern community. The Pickax police chief, Andrew Brodie, was the first to hear about the car crash. It had occurred four hundred miles to the south, in the perilous urban area that locals called Down Below. The metropolitan police appealed to Brodie for assistance in locating the next of kin. . . . The driver's body was consumed by the flames, but through the license plates the registration had been traced to James Qwilleran. . . ."

12. "It was late October, and Moose County, 400 miles north of everywhere, was in danger of being wiped off the map. In the grip of a record-breaking drought, towns and farms and forests could be reduced to ashes overnight—given a spark and a high wind. Volunteer firefighters were on round-the-clock alert, and the congregations of fourteen churches prayed for snow. Not rain. Snow! Winter always began with a three-day blizzard, called the Big One, that buried everything under snow drifting to ten feet. . . . Late one evening, in a condominium northeast of Pickax City, the county seat, a cat sat on a windowsill, stretching his neck, raising his nose and sniffing. The man watching him thought, he smells a skunk. They had recently moved to the wooded area with its new sights, sounds, new smells."

13. "It was a weekend in June—glorious weather for boating. A small cabin cruiser with *Double-Six* freshly painted on the sternboard

chugged across the lake at a cautious speed. Stowed on the aft deck were suitcases, cartons, a turkey roaster without handles, and a small wire-mesh cage with a jacket thrown over the top. . . . Pointing across the water to a thick black line on the horizon, the pilot announced loudly, 'That's our destination. . . .' "

14. "Jim Qwilleran slumped in a chair in the Press Club dining room, his six-feet-two telescoped into a picture of dejection and his morose expression intensified by the droop of his oversized moustache. . . . Qwilleran had been stunned by bad news of a more vital nature. . . . Qwilleran continued to stare at the sheet of green paper, adjusting his new reading glasses on his nose as if he couldn't believe they were telling him the truth. . . . In silence Qwilleran finished reading his incredible document and started again at the top of the list: No Potatoes, No Bread, No Cream Soup, No Fried Foods. . . ."

15. "In December the weather declared war. First it bombarded the city with ice storms, then strafed it with freezing winds. Now it was snowing belligerently. A blizzard whipped down Canard Street, past the Press Club. . . . With malicious accuracy the largest flakes zeroed in to make cold wet landings on the neck of the man who was hailing a taxi in front of the club. . . . When a cab pulled to the curb, he eased himself carefully into the back seat . . . and gave the driver the name of a third-rate hotel. 'Medford Manor? Let's see, I can take Zwinger Street and the expressway,' the cabbie said hopefully as he threw the flag on the meter. . . ."

QUICK
ASSOCIATIONS

Which mystery in the series do you associate with the following?

1. UFOs in Mooseville.

2. The restoration of an old steam locomotive.

3. The Highland Games.

4. Qwill covers the interior design beat for the *Daily Fluxion*.

5. Koko develops a strange fondness for classical music.

6. Qwill begins a diet and creates a new gourmet column.

7. A stabbing in an art gallery and vandalized paintings.

8. The Great Food Explo.

9. The local newspaper publisher perishes in an accident.

10. Qwill moves into the Gage mansion and unearths some skeletons.

11. Qwill inherits millions and moves into a mansion.

12. Yum Yum comes to live with Qwill and Koko.

13. Qwill and the cats vacation at his log cabin in Moose County.

14. Qwill and the cats attempt to solve a mystery in a historic farmhouse.

15. Qwill is off to Scotland.

16. The Casablanca building is in danger of demolition.

17. A rich banker and his wife are killed.

18. A real estate developer is pushed off a cliff.

19. Hilary VanBrook, the principal of Pickax High School, is found dead.

20. A record-breaking drought is complicated by a rash of fires at historic mine sites.

THE CAT WHO COULD READ BACKWARDS

General Questions

1. When we first meet Qwill, where is he living?

2. What is the circulation of the *Daily Fluxion*?

3. What is the publisher's slogan?

4. Where does Qwill first meet Koko?

5. For whom is Koko named?

Chronological Order of Events

Arrange the following events in their order of occurrence.

_____ Qwill discovers Mountclemens's body on the patio.

_____ Earl Lambreth's body is discovered.

_____ The Ghirotto painting of the ballet dancer is missing from the Lambreth Gallery.

_____ Koko leads Qwill to a heavy wall tapestry, which hides a door that leads to the downstairs apartment.

_____ Koko sniffs at a closet door, and when Qwill opens it, he discovers racks holding paintings.

_____ Qwill discovers the missing half of the Ghirotto.

_____ A portrait of a blue robot, signed by O. Narx, is discovered.

_____ Qwill returns to the downstairs apartment and discovers that two pictures of robots are missing.

_____ Koko reads the signature, Scrano, from left to right.

_____ Qwill hits Narx with a flashlight.

🐾 Koko

1. Koko likes white grape juice.   True or False?

2. Koko refuses to eat raw meat.   True or False?

3. Koko does not like modern art.   True or False?

4. Koko is suspicious of strangers.   True or False?

🐾 Women in Qwill's Life

1. Qwill takes this "lyrically tall and lovely" lady out to dinner a couple of times. She has straight, dark hair, two children, and is married to Cal. What is her name?

2. After her husband's murder, Qwill wonders how long it will be before he can invite this lady out to dinner. Who is she?

🐾 Qwill's Living Quarters

1. When Qwill moves into one of Mountclemens's apartments, what does he complain about?

2. What famous painter's work hangs over the mantel in the apartment that Qwill rents from Mountclemens?

🐾 Dining Out
Match the food and the place.

a. Sitting Bull's Chop House   b. The Artist and Model
c. Mountclemens's kitchen

1. Lobster bisque, Caesar salad, chicken livers and bacon enbrochette

2. Ragout de boeuf Bordelaise

3. Chopped sirloin, gigantic lamb chops, and cheesecake

Crimes and Victims

1. Who killed Lambreth?

2. Who killed Mountclemens?

3. How was Lambreth killed?

THE CAT WHO ATE DANISH MODERN

 General Questions

1. What is the name of the magazine Qwill is asked to produce?

2. Qwill receives some early advice from decorator David Lyke. Complete his advice to Qwill:

   "Never call d_____ d_____."

3. According to George Tait, what is the rarest color of jade?

4. After Qwill is evicted from his apartment at Mountclemens's, where does he move?

5. What is Qwill's apartment number?

6. Complete the following words flushed out by Koko while playing the Dictionary Game:

   b_____, s____r_____c, r_____la,
   k____l_____.

7. Mrs. Tait's maiden name was _____.

 Chronological Order of Events
Arrange the following events in their order of occurrence.

_____ Mrs. Tait is found dead by her husband.

_____ Koko licks the photograph of the Biedermeier armoire.

_____ Mr. Tait discovers his jade collection is missing.

_____ Qwill discovers the secret panel with the missing jade inside.

_____ Koko finds the word _sacroiliac_ twice in one week.

_____ Tait attacks Qwill with a spike.

_____ Bunsen finds David Lyke, dead of a bullet wound in his chest.

_____ Natalie Noyton takes her own life.

_____ Koko is honored for his part in solving the crime.

_____ Qwill receives his new assignment to publish a weekly magazine on interior design.

Koko and Yum Yum

1. Koko's eyes are blue.   True or False?

2. Qwill thinks Koko can read price tags.   True or False?

3. What does Mrs. Tait call Yum Yum?

4. What does Mr. Tait insist Yum Yum's name is?

5. Place a K before those qualities that belong to Koko and a Y before those belonging to Yum Yum.

_____ Likes to lick glue.   _____ Eyes are violet blue.
_____ Has a cowlick.   _____ Has an honorary press card.
_____ Has a kink in the tail.

Women in Qwill's Life

1. Who does Qwill meet and dance with at the Photographers' Ball?

2. Qwill meets Alacoque Wright. Arrange in chronological order the dates Qwill has with Cokey.

_____ Cokey invites Qwill to her apartment for dinner. Cokey chases him out early because they both have to work the next day.

_____ On Saturday Qwill takes Cokey to the ballpark.

_____ Qwill takes Cokey to the Press Club.

_____ Qwill takes Cokey to a party at Villa Verandah.

_____ Qwill takes Cokey to his apartment. Koko is clearly jealous and reacts accordingly.

3. Since Koko is jealous of Cokey, what does Cokey suggest that Qwill call her in order not to upset Koko?

Qwill's Living Quarters

1. Villa Verandah is also known as _____ _____.

2. How many stories are there in the apartment building in which Qwill lives?

3. Who was the previous occupant of the apartment in which Qwill lives?

4. David Lyke described Noyton's apartment as "tastefully done in wall-to-wall money." Noyton, on the other hand, described it as "_____."

Dining Out

At the Villa Verandah, "It was not the bar that interested Qwilleran. It was the buffet. It was laden with . . ."

1. Can you unscramble the items that appeared on the buffet menu?

Cvraai	Llsaabemt
Srmhip	Athkoecri htsrea
Rreatib	Lldi ausce
Msshrmoou	

2. "I'll make us one of nature's own cocktails if you'll order the ingredients and two champagne glasses." What are the ingredients needed in order to make "nature's own cocktail"?

Crimes and Victims

1. Who killed David Lyke?

2. How was Lyke killed?

3. What happens to Natalie Noyton?

THE CAT WHO TURNED ON AND OFF

General Questions

1. Qwill has moved again. Where does he live now?

2. What is Qwill's apartment room number?

3. What were the prizes for the annual writing contest?

4. The inscription, "*Touch not the catt bot a glove,*" appears on what object Qwill spots in the Blue Dragon antique shop?

5. Who bought the finial on which Glanz was supposedly impaled?

6. What is Mary Duckworth's real name?

7. What did Qwill and Mary find hidden under the wallpaper that was peeled back in Andy's room?

8. How did the junkies identify themselves?

9. Which key on the typewriter originally belonging to Andrew Glanz was missing?

🐾 Chronological Order of Events
Arrange the following events in their order of occurrence.

_____ C. C. Cobb dies while scrounging at the Ellsworth House.

_____ Mrs. McGuffey tells Qwill that Andy was writing a novel.

_____ Qwill invites Ben to his apartment for a drink and to toast the season.

_____ Andrew Glanz dies.

_____ Koko wanders in the hall and discovers the finial upon which Glanz is supposedly impaled.

_____ Qwill visits Ben's apartment and comes across a stiff blond hair.

_____ Koko leads Qwill and Mary to the discovery of the hidden passageway.

_____ Koko rubs his jaw against the latch on the ashpit of the pot-bellied stove.

_____ Qwill finds a small packet of drugs on the floor.

_____ Koko turns the tape recorder on, and Ben hears C. C. accusing him of selling drugs.

_____ The Mackintosh coat of arms falls from the mantel and knocks Ben down.

_____ Ben confesses to killing Andy Glanz and pushing C. C. Cobb down the stairs.

🐾 Koko and Yum Yum

1. Where do Koko and Yum Yum sleep in Qwill's apartment at Medford Manor?

2. How do Koko and Yum Yum like to wake Qwill up?

3. To which side of Koko does Yum Yum sit?

😺 Women in Qwill's Life

1. From whom does Qwill receive a letter in which there is a "graceless hint for money?"

2. Qwill also receives a "note written in brown ink with feminine flourishes. . . ." From whom is this note?

3. Mary Duckworth and Cluthra both pursue Qwill in *The Cat Who Turned On and Off*. Place an M in front of the statements that relate to Mary Duckworth and a C in front of those relating to Cluthra.

   _____ Invites Qwill to Skyline Towers.

   _____ Has "large dark eyes, heavily rimmed with black pencil . . ."

   _____ Qwill considers her a potential date for the Christmas Eve party at the Press Club.

   _____ Koko's reaction to this lady is "not hostile—only unflattering."

   _____ Sneezes repeatedly and leaves abruptly.

😺 Qwill's Living Quarters

1. Medford Manor is also known as _____ _____.

2. To where does Qwill move after leaving Medford Manor?

3. Which furniture belongs where? Use MM if the furniture belongs in Qwill's room at Medford Manor and TJ if it is in the Cobbs' apartment.

   _____ Double bed with limp fringe on the bedspread

   _____ A daybed "built like a swan boat"

   _____ An armchair

   _____ "High-backed gilded chairs with seats supported by gargoyles"

   _____ A patterned rug

   _____ "Built-in bookshelves filled with volumes in old leather"

   _____ "Closet door standing ajar"

4. Who built the Cobb mansion?

5. What was the original purpose of the passageway that the cats discover?

6. What is the name of the ghost that supposedly lives in the Cobbs' mansion?

🐾 Dining Out

1. Iris Cobb invites Qwill to "have dinner with us around seven o'clock, and then you won't have to go out of the house. . . ." Unscramble the menu so you can see what Iris served Qwill.

Cbrnarrye uijce ktlccaio	Mshdea pttsaooe
Rpshkioi	Dlsaa htwi rftoueqor gnissedr
Top tsoar	Ccontuo ceak

2. When Qwill visits the shop of the Three Weird Sisters, what do they offer him to eat?

3. Qwill enjoys pink lemonade and Christmas cookies with the Women's Department. True or False?

4. Mary tells Qwill that she took the liberty of ordering dinner for Christmas Eve and that it was being sent over from the Toledo Restaurant. What did she order?

5. What does Mary give the cats for Christmas?

🐾 Crimes and Victims

1. Who killed Andrew Glanz? Why?

2. Who killed C. C. Cobb?

3. Did Ben admit killing the man in the alley?

THE CAT WHO
SAW RED

🐾 General Questions

1. How many pounds does Dr. Beane tell Qwill to lose?

2. According to Joy Graham, what is Qwill's favorite liquor?

3. Koko frequently left a clue for Qwill on paper in the typewriter. Arrange these clues in their order of appearance:

____ PB	____ dog
____ 30	____ Z
____ T	

4. Whose initials were on the bottom of the bean pot used by Mrs. Marron?

5. What is the name of Qwill's new column?

🐾 Chronological Order of Events
Arrange the following events in their order of occurrence.

____ Qwill is awakened by a loud scream.

____ Koko finds "a small glazed ceramic piece the size and shape of a beetle" while walking near the river.

_____ Qwill sees a convertible pull away from the building.

_____ Koko jumps to a table and rubs his nose on a pot with a red living glaze.

_____ In the clay room, Koko is fascinated by a trapdoor in the floor.

_____ Koko sharpens his nails on a notebook.

_____ Koko pushes a red library book to the floor for a second time.

_____ Koko types 30.

_____ William fails to show up to go to the market with Qwill and Robert.

_____ Qwill discovers a book with a red cover lying on the floor.

_____ Koko and Yum Yum tilt pictures in the apartment.

_____ Qwill peers through a hole in the wall and sees Dan Graham "copying from a loose-leaf notebook into a large ledger."

_____ Qwill is awakened by "the fall of a body, the crash of a chair, the crack of a head hitting the ceramic tile floor, the shattering of a window."

_____ Qwill and Bunsen go to Graham's apartment to take pictures for a feature article.

_____ Qwill discovers a wall patch behind a slanted picture.

_____ Dan Graham tells Qwill that Joy has left.

_____ Mrs. Marron sees a man coming down the fire escape that leads to the Grahams' loft.

_____ Dan gives Qwill a pot coated with the living glaze.

🐾 Koko and Yum Yum

1. How does Koko signal to Qwill that he is ready for breakfast?

2. Regarding Koko's and Yum Yum's eating habits, Qwill suggests that "If there's _____ in there, they won't eat chicken; and if there's _____, they won't eat _____."

Women in Qwill's Life

1. Joy and Qwill were once engaged. True or False?

2. After Joy left Chicago, where did she go?

3. How much money does Qwill loan Joy?

4. Who accompanies Qwill to Rattlesnake Lodge?

5. Who is who? Which characteristics describe Joy, and which describe Rosemary? Use J or R to identify the appropriate characteristics.

   _____ Qwill finds "her company relaxing."

   _____ She volunteers to massage Qwill's neck.

   _____ She has lived in California and Florida.

   _____ "They were engaged a long time ago, until she suddenly left town."

   _____ A "nice-looking woman of indefinite age and quiet manner."

   _____ A "tiny figure, heavy chestnut hair, and a provocative one-sided smile."

Qwill's Living Quarters

1. What is Qwill's room number at Maus Haus?

2. On what street is Maus Haus?

3. The rent is higher on Zwinger Street than at Maus Haus. True or False?

4. What was Maus Haus before Robert Maus took possession of it?

Dining Out

1. This restaurant, a "series of cavernous rooms, long and narrow . . ." offers "acquavit to zabaglione. . . ." Qwill and Robert Maus enjoy French onion soup, eels in green sauce, veal and mushrooms, braised fennel almandine, salad and chestnut puree here. What is the name of this restaurant?

2. This restaurant was once the depot for interurban trolleys. Name it and unscramble some of the food items on the menu.

Ssseoiyhciv   Rehgnir ni rsuo rcmea
Cark fo bmla   Nnaaab baaarinv

3. Where did Qwill eat the following? MH for Maus Haus, PB for the Petrified Bagel, TT for Toledo Tombs, RI for Rattlesnake Inn, and FF for Friendly Fatties.

_____ Stuffed breast of chicken baked in a crust

_____ A "frozen hamburger, gently warmed, and some canned peas"

_____ Avocado supreme remoulade

_____ Asparagus that ". . . tasted like Brussels sprouts . . ."

_____ Cabbage juice cocktails

_____ Brussels sprouts that tasted "like wet papier-mâché"

_____ Corn chowder

4. While at Maus Haus, Qwill attends a demonstration dinner where "everybody cooks something at the table." Can you match the cook with what he/she cooked? Hixie Rice (HR), Mrs. Marron (MM), Charlotte Roop (CR), Rosemary (R), and Sorrel (S).

_____ Steak au poivre

_____ "Cold soup involving yogurt, cucumbers, dill and raisins"

_____ A tossed salad

_____ "Potato puffs and asparagus garnished with pimento strips"

_____ Cherries jubilee

Crimes and Victims

1. How was Joy killed?

2. Who killed Joy and why?

3. Who killed William and how?

THE CAT WHO PLAYED BRAHMS

 General Questions

1. What color of car did Qwill buy? What was the significance of the measurements "fourteen by sixteen?"

2. According to his eviction notice, when must he be out of Maus Haus?

3. According to Qwill, how old will Aunt Fanny be "next month"?

4. What is Percy's proposed new position for Qwill at the *Fluxion*?

5. What does the bartender predict will happen to Qwill after drinking so much tomato juice?

6. According to Qwill, who wears "flashy clothes and bright lipstick, and has a voice like a drill sergeant . . . [and] is spunky and bossy and full of energy and ideas"?

7. According to Qwill, how many documents were in Aunt Fanny's safe? What were they?

8. In order for Qwill to inherit Aunt Fanny's fortune, what must he do?

9. Which will is which? Qwill discovers three wills in Fanny's safe.

Which will is the oldest? Which is second in the series? And which one is the final will?

_____ This will "bequeathed half of her estate to the Atlantic City foundation and the other half to the schools, churches, cultural and charitable organizations, health care facilities, and civic causes in Pickax City."

_____ This will "bequeathed Fanny's entire estate to a foundation in Atlantic City. . . ."

_____ This will "leaves the sum of one dollar to each of the beneficiaries heretofore named . . ." and the rest to Qwill.

Chronological Order of Events
Arrange the following events in their order of occurrence.

_____ Rosemary buys tulips from the prison gift shop.

_____ Buck Dunfield is beaten to death.

_____ While sitting on the moose head, Koko manages to free a cassette tape from behind the head.

_____ Qwill's expensive gold watch disappears.

_____ Qwill goes fishing with the Whatleys.

_____ Koko leads Qwill and Rosemary to the toolshed.

_____ Qwill catches something that "looked like the body of a man. . . ."

_____ Koko uncovers a large manila envelope under the blanket on Tom's cot.

_____ Penelope Goodwinter calls to inform Qwill that Aunt Fanny has fallen down a flight of stairs and died.

_____ Nick Bamba explains to Qwill about the "ferry racket."

_____ Rosemary tells Qwill that the man at the turkey farm has a money clip like one Qwill found at the cabin.

_____ Qwill finds Tom's body in the shed.

_____ Tom confesses to killing Aunt Fanny.

_____ Qwill realizes that Hanstable's voice is on the tape.

_____ Tom explains that Hanstable told him to buy whisky for the prisoners.

Koko and Yum Yum

1. As Qwill heads for his north country vacation, which cat howls "in strident tones whenever the car turned a corner, rounded a curve, crossed a bridge, passed under a viaduct, encountered a truck, or exceeded fifty miles an hour"?

2. Once at the cabin, which cat "sits imperiously on the moose head"?

3. Which cat likes to untie guests' shoelaces?

4. Both cats become weather forecasters. Use K to indicate what Koko does to predict the weather, and Y for those things Yum Yum does.

    _____ Runs into the legs of tables and chairs

    _____ Lets out "earsplitting howls" and "an occasional shriek"

5. When Rosemary returns to the cabin with tulips of different colors, which cat pulls out the black ones and scatters them on the floor?

6. Which cat maneuvers its tail under Rosemary's feet as she walks around the cabin?

Women in Qwill's Life

1. Two women figure prominently in Qwill's life while he's at the north country cabin. Who are they?

2. Who is Qwill describing when he says she is "enjoyable company" but refers "to his age too frequently"?

3. Who, according to Qwill, is "an attractive brunette with a youthful figure" and fun to have around?

4. Who locks Koko in the bathroom after he scatters black tulips over the floor for a second time?

5. Qwill admits that "he was not entirely sorry to see her [Rosemary]

move to Toronto." Check all the reasons he gives for his feeling this way.

_____ He has been a bachelor for too long.

_____ He couldn't adjust to someone restricting what he eats.

_____ He doesn't like knickknacks.

_____ He gave up the pipe for her.

_____ She wasn't attractive and seldom compassionate.

_____ He often found younger women more stimulating.

_____ She "was not tuned in to his sense of humor. . . ."

_____ She "was certainly not tuned in to Koko."

🐾 Qwill's Living Quarters

In this story Qwill spends time at Aunt Fanny's cabin "on the lake, about four hundred miles north. Near Mooseville," and visits Aunt Fanny at her "large, square fieldstone mansion."

1. Can you unscramble objects found in Aunt Fanny's "large, square fieldstone mansion"?

   Glhseni upb   Eeldpna blrryai
   Ggoeianr rvlsie   Drnga esacrstia
   Ffatssrdoerih clltniooec

2. Now can you unscramble the objects found in Aunt Fanny's cabin "on the lake, about four hundred miles north. Near Mooseville"?

   Hdmooseae   Ploowhlir htba
   Eeednscr sehcrpo   Pdxeoes sogl
   Eioenstfld mnyhcie

🐾 Dining Out

Qwill eats in several different establishments while in Mooseville. Can you match the place to his menu selections? One place is used twice. Places: Northern Lights Hotel, FOO, Nasty Pasty, Old Stone Mill, Dimsdale Diner

1. Here he ate "mediocre pork chops, a soggy baked potato, overcooked green beans . . . and gelatinous blueberry pie."

2. Pasties here are a "foot wide and three inches thick."

3. This establishment is a "boxcar punctuated with windows of various sorts." Its speciality is goulash with coleslaw.

4. Qwill finds an ordinary menu here, and while dining with Rosemary, he suggests that she try the chicken julienne salad, which consists of "tired lettuce and imitation tomatoes . . . invisible chicken . . . bottled dressing from Kansas City and a dusting of Parmesan that tastes like sawdust."

5. Here the dinner menu offers "Nova Scotia halibut, Columbia River salmon, and Boston scrod."

6. The pasties here are "flaky, have a little sauce and less turnip."

7. What does Qwill consider the "Moose County Specialty?"

Crimes and Victims

1. Who kills Buck Dunfield? How is he killed?

2. How does Qwill identify Hanstable as the murderer?

3. How did Hanstable smuggle the whisky into the prison?

4. Why did Hanstable kill Dunfield?

5. What was the "ferry racket"?

6. Why does Tom commit suicide?

CHARACTER IDENTIFICATION I

Who is who? Can you identify the following characters?

1. Owner of residence for professional girls.

2. Church editor of the *Fluxion.*

3. Name the three sisters who run the Three Weird Sisters antique shop.

4. Roger MacGillivray's mother-in-law.

5. Assistant to Mrs. Middy, and a.k.a. Cokey.

6. Women's editor of the *Daily Fluxion.*

7. A *Thingist,* this artist makes "meaningful constructions out of junk and calls them Things."

8. History teacher who during the summer works at the Tourist Development Association in Mooseville.

9. Co-owner with Starkweather of the largest decorating firm in Junktown.

10. A "psycatatrist" who is not a real doctor but rather "a cat fancier with a bit of common sense."

11. Detective from the homicide division Down Below.

12. Antique dealer who died when he fell from a ladder onto a finial.

13. Owner of the Blue Dragon antique shop in Junktown. She is also known as The Dragon.

14. Antique dealer who is killed while scrounging for materials in an abandoned house. Iris is his wife.

15. Managing editor of the *Daily Fluxion*. He frequently uses the phrase "per se."

16. Police reporter and the *Fluxion*'s regular man at police headquarters.

17. Superb cook, avid collector, and an attorney. The Gourmet Club meets in his home.

18. Robert Maus's housekeeper.

19. A "nice-looking woman of indefinite age and quiet manner . . ." Her husband died two years ago; she sold their house and invested the money in a health-food store.

20. Famous abolitionist who built the Cobb mansion.

21. Owner of the Golden Lamb Chop.

22. Manager of the Heavenly Hash House in Midwest City.

23. Arch Riker's first wife.

24. This person, an artist of robots in Junktown, is the same person as Scrano.

25. Art critic for the *Daily Fluxion* and quite a gourmet cook.

26. Retired schoolteacher who taught Andy Glanz to read. She owns a Junktown antique shop, the Piggin, Noggin and Firkin.

27. Wealthy man who lives in the Muggy Swamp area and owner of a jade collection.

28. Photographer for the *Daily Fluxion*. He likes a martini "without the garbage in it."

29. A potter and one of Qwill's old flames.

30. Resident of Mooseville who has an "idiopathic stink." He runs the turkey farm on Pickax Road.

CLUES, CLUES, CLUES I

Can you identify the mystery based on the list of clues provided?

1. Biedermeier armoire
   Missing jade button
   Yellowish pink wool with metallic threads
   Dictionary words: *sacroiliac, sadism, rubeola, frame, ruddiness*

   _____

2. Ballet dancer
   Racks holding paintings
   Heavy wall tapestry
   Blue robot
   Knife rack

   _____

3. Finial
   Stiff blond hair
   Underground Railroad passage
   Drugs
   Portable tape recorder

Coat of arms
Manuscript of unfinished novel

_____

4. Gold pen
   Coral lipstick
   Moose head
   Candlesticks
   Whisky
   Torn ear and scratches
   Black tulips
   Gold money clip

_____

5. Convertible
   Ceramic pieces
   Initials "J. G."
   "30"
   Book with red cover
   Plumbum (Pb)
   Red urn
   Lead oxide
   Kiln

_____

PLACES, PLACES, PLACES I

How many places do you remember from your reading? See how many you can identify.

1. This is the street on which the Press Club is located.

2. This is the term used by the residents of Mooseville to refer to areas to the south.

3. The county of which Pickax City is the county seat.

4. An exclusive neighborhood Down Below where residents live in French chateaux and English manor style homes.

5. The most expensive restaurant Down Below. It has two names.

6. Small restaurant with the "second worst coffee in Moose County."

7. Lakeside eating establishment that lost the D in its name. Famous for pasties.

8. This restaurant, a "dilapidated boxcar," has the "worst coffee in the county and the worst hamburgers in the northeast central United States."

9. Junktown antique shop owned by Mary Duckworth.

10. Antique shop owned by Iris and C. C. Cobb.

11. Art gallery in an old loft building near the financial district Down Below.

12. A hotel where Qwill takes a room. It is also known as Medicare Manor.

13. High-rise apartment building, shaped like a waffle, also known as Architect's Revenge.

14. Hotel in Mooseville, a "relic from the 1860s." It resembles "a shoe-box with windows."

QWILL QUIZ 1

How much have you learned about James Qwilleran already? Take the quiz and find out!

1. What is Qwill's full name?

2. How tall is he?

3. In which month and on what day was Qwill born?

4. Where was Qwill born?

5. What did Qwill's mother call him?

6. What was Qwill's mother's name, and where was she born?

7. What was Qwill's mother reading when he was born?

8. As a kid, what two things did Qwill hate?

9. What did Qwill's school friends call him?

10. What was the name of Qwill's high school newspaper and what position did he have on the newspaper staff?

11. When Qwill went to college, what did he intend to become?

12. Name one of four plays Qwill participated in while in college.

13. During his senior year in college, Qwill was employed as a bartender. True or False?

14. Qwill met his future wife while in England. True or False?

15. What was Qwill's wife's name? How long have they been divorced?

THE CAT WHO HAD
14 TALES

In *The Cat Who Had 14 Tales* we are introduced to several felines who also exhibit remarkable catly behaviors, often reminding us of Koko and/or Yum Yum.

A. How many of these cats can you identify? Select from this list: Percy, Marmalade, Dahk Won, Tipsy, Sin-Sin, Drooler, Shadow, SuSu, Whiskers, Spook, Madam Phloi, Conscience/Constance, Phut Phat, and Stanley.

1. This Siamese communicates by staring at his owners' foreheads until they get the message.

2. This cat is the mouser for the Lockmaster Museum.

3. This silver tabby talks to visiting ghosts.

4. This cat appears on the cover of a national magazine.

5. This Siamese disconnects the coffeemaker with her teeth; turns on the television in the middle of the night; flushes the toilet hourly; and opens the milk chute, enabling the town's tomcat population to come in.

6. This Siamese likes to sit inside the grand piano.

7. This cat lived at Nick's Market, Sam's Drugstore, and Gus's Timber-lake Bar before settling at Tipsy's Tavern.

8. This cat is black with white feet and green eyes and lives in a bank.

9. This is an unusual pair of cats.

10. A foundation to study the mental perception of the domestic feline will be named after this cat.

11. This blond cat is clumsy, for a cat.

12. This Siamese likes to watch pigeons, listen to ghosts of deceased mice, and shake a paw at cheese she doesn't like.

13. A sleek black cat who helps solve the mystery of Mary Sloan.

14. This cat can fly straight up like a helicopter.

B. Now can you match the cat and the story/mystery?

Who belongs where?

    _____ 1. "The Sin of Madame Phloi"
    _____ 2. "Stanley and Spook"
    _____ 3. "Tragedy on New Year's Eve"
    _____ 4. "The Hero of Drummond Street"
    _____ 5. "The Mad Museum Mouser"
    _____ 6. "The Fluppie Phenomenon"
    _____ 7. "Tipsy and the Board of Health"
    _____ 8. "A Cat Named Conscience"
    _____ 9. "SuSu and the 8:30 Ghost"
    _____ 10. "Weekend of the Big Puddle"

THE CAT WHO PLAYED POST OFFICE

🐾 General Questions

1. When the story opens, where is Qwill? What has happened to him?

2. How long has it been since Qwill lived in Chicago?

3. If Qwill forfeits the inheritance from Aunt Fanny, who gets it?

4. How many people does Qwill interview for the housekeeper's position before he receives Iris Cobb's letter of inquiry?

5. Why is there no whistling in Pickax?

6. How far is Pickax City from Mooseville?

7. What do the locals, in Pickax parlance, refer to as the "urban sprawl in the southern half of the state"?

8. How does Qwill propose to resolve the issue of the flag in the council's chamber?

9. Who suggests that Qwill purchase the *Picayune*?

10. Qwill discovers no Mulls in the fourteen-page Pickax telephone book, but how many Goodwinters does he find?

☙ Chronological Order of Events

Arrange the following events in their order of occurrence.

_____ Koko paws at the graffiti while attempting to reach one set of initials: S. G.

_____ Koko leads Qwill and Melinda to the attic, where they find a carton with a tag with Daisy Mull's name on it.

_____ Koko plays the tune "Daisy, Daisy" on the piano.

_____ Daisy Mull's mother dies and is found in her trailer home.

_____ Koko finds Daisy's notebook between the bed and the wall.

_____ Mrs. Cobb reports that things are moving "around mysteriously" in the kitchen.

_____ Koko plays the opening phrase of "Three Blind Mice" on the piano.

_____ Tiffany Trotter talks about Daisy.

_____ The cats' metal commode is in the middle of the floor, and Koko is "preparing to give it another shove with his nose."

_____ Mildred translates the diary for Qwill.

_____ Qwill wakes up in the hospital after a truck swerves "down upon him and his rickety bicycle."

_____ Koko awakens Qwill. Koko races down the stairs; Qwill follows and hears the back door opening.

_____ Penelope commits suicide by running her car in the closed garage.

_____ Penelope's letter tells about the affair between Alexander and Daisy.

_____ Qwill learns that Daisy is buried a thousand feet underground at the Three Pines Mine.

🐾 Koko and Yum Yum

1. On which step of the staircase does Koko prefer to sit?

2. Who likes to push mail under the oriental rug?

3. What tunes does Koko play on the piano?

4. From whom does Qwill receive a letter addressed to him in red ink?

🐾 Women in Qwill's Life

1. She has a "dazzling smile and provocative dimples" but when Qwill asks her out to dinner she declines. Who is this?

2. Koko makes it clear to Melinda that it is time to go. Place in order the subtle—or not so subtle—hints he gives her when it's time to go.

   _____ He stops at intervals and looks to see if she is following him. In the hallway he stares "pointedly at the door handle."

   _____ He walks in, utters an "imperious YOW!" Then goes to the hallway and stares at the front door.

   _____ Koko walks into the library and stares hard at Melinda, then marches to the front door and stares at it.

3. Penelope or Melinda? Who is who? Place P in front of the statements that describe Penelope, and M in front of those that describe Melinda.

   _____ Attorney.

   _____ Doctor.

   _____ She reads Qwill's columns and quotes him as if he were Shakespeare.

   _____ "Attractive green eyes and the longest eyelashes."

   _____ "Conspicuously well dressed for a town like Pickax."

   _____ She has been dating Qwill for two months.

Qwill's Living Quarters

1. How many windows does the K Mansion have?

2. What does Qwill call the carriage house at the rear of the K Mansion?

3. How many people will the dining room seat?

4. Which room has "William and Mary banister-back chairs surrounding a dark oak table, and yellow and green chintz covering the walls and draping the windows"?

5. Which room offers a "wraparound coziness" and the "warm colors of Bokhara rugs" and "leather seating"?

6. How many fireplaces and chandeliers are there in the drawing room?

7. Match the suite to its furnishings: French (F), Biedermeier (B), Empire (E), and Old English (OE)

   _____ This suite has a "Norman bonnet-top armoire."

   _____ In this suite there are "enough sphinxes and gryphons to cause nightmares."

   _____ Here you'll find "Chippendale highboys and lowboys and a canopied bed." Qwill chooses this as his bedroom.

   _____ If painted flowers are your preference, then this suite will suit you.

8. There are two apartments in the carriage house. One apartment has drab walls and shabby furniture. The other, however, has walls and ceiling covered with what?

Dining Out

1. This restaurant serves a "twelve-ounce bacon cheeseburger with fries," the so-called "Cholesterol Special." Is it the Hotel Booze Dining Room or Otto's Tasty Eats?

2. What is the specialty of the house at The Old Stone Mill? Hint: They "buy it frozen and it's the only thing on the menu that the cook can't ruin."

3. After dining at this restaurant, Qwill persuades the kitchen to "*broil* two orders of pickerel *without breading.*" This family restaurant has a "smoking section" and a "screaming section."

4. What is the name of the Lanspeaks' new restaurant? For whom is it named?

5. While eating at the Lanspeaks' restaurant, Qwill and Melinda order trout almandine and asparagus. Instead of asparagus, what do they receive?

🐾 The Klingenschoen Mansion Dinner Party

Qwill decides to give a dinner party. Melinda consents to be his hostess, "or any-thing else. . . ." She suggests "six courses . . . a butler serving cocktails . . . two footmen to serve in the dining room. . . ."

6. Can you unscramble the menu suggested by Melinda?

   According to Melinda, Qwill ". . . ought to serve foods indigenous to this area, starting with TRRNEIE FO TNAASEHP and DLLJEEI CRSSETERWA MMEONOSC. . . . How about . . . MONSAL TTCOQRUESE for the fish course?" . . . "the entrée could be BLMA UCHBONNREE with tiny Moose County TOEPSTOA NDA SHRMOOSMU . . . then a salad of homegrown AAASPRSGU GTTVNAIIERE . . . [And] don't forget dessert. . . . How about a wild RYERBPRSA TFLEIR?"

🐾 Crimes and Victims

1. How does Della Mull die?

2. How did Daisy Mull die?

3. Who killed Della Mull, Daisy Mull, and Tiffany Trotter?

4. How does Alexander die?

THE CAT WHO
KNEW SHAKESPEARE

🐾 **General Questions**

1. During which month does this story take place?

2. What did Qwill manage to save from the Klingenschoen Museum fire?

3. The Klingenschoen Mansion is one of five important buildings sitting on Park Circle. What are the other four?

4. Whose portrait hung inside the lobby of the public library?

5. Who built Mrs. Cobb's mobile herb garden?

6. What happened to Polly's husband?

7. Who is William Allen?

8. Who are the principals in XYZ Enterprises?

9. Koko is on "a Shakespeare kick." Can you arrange in their order the books Koko pushes from the shelves?

_____ *Macbeth*   _____ *Julius Caesar*
_____ *King Henry VIII*   _____ *Othello*
_____ *Hamlet*   _____ *The Tempest*
_____ *A Midsummer Night's Dream*

🐾 Chronological Order of Events

Arrange the following events in their order of occurrence.

_____ Senior Goodwinter is killed.

_____ The Klingenschoen Museum is destroyed by fire.

_____ The *Picayune* newspaper building burns to the ground.

_____ Gertrude Goodwinter and Harry Noyton are killed on Airport Road.

_____ Junior and Jody fly Down Below to get married.

_____ Qwill entertains the Historical Society and Old Timers Club at K Mansion.

_____ Qwill interviews Euphonia Gage, President of the Old Timers Club.

_____ Qwill tells Junior about his plan to get Noyton to buy the paper and to bring Riker on board as publisher and Junior as editor.

_____ Noyton calls Qwill to tell him that the Goodwinter deal to buy the *Picayune* is "sewed up."

_____ Mrs. Cobb and Herb Hackpole, a.k.a. Basil Whittelstaff, are married.

_____ Mrs. Cobb comes back to the mansion, "her face haggard and drained of color."

_____ Qwill learns that Hackpole is the arsonist.

_____ Junior discovers that his father has been putting a hundred years of the *Picayune* on microfilm, and he didn't want anyone to know he was spending the money.

_____ Hixie tells Qwill that the unidentified body in the car stuck in the snowdrift was Tony. She also tells Qwill that she has been invited to go along with Exbridge on a Carribbean cruise.

_____ Qwill decides to construct a theater on the site of the charred ruins of the Klingenschoen Mansion.

🐾 Koko and Yum Yum

Again in this story, Koko and Yum Yum are up to their usual tricks. However, they also exhibit new talents, which surprise even Qwill. Which cat does the following? Koko (K) or Yum Yum (Y)?

_____ Pushing secondhand books off the shelves

_____ Having telephone conversations with Lori Bamba

_____ Riding up the elevator while carrying a dead mouse

_____ Batting Iris Cobb's wedding ring around and pushing it under a rug

_____ "Carrying on like a banshee" prior to the fire at the K Mansion

🐾 Women in Qwill's Life

In The Cat Who Knew Shakespeare, *we meet Polly Duncan for the first time. What do we learn about Polly?*

1. Where does she work? What is her position there?

2. How long has she lived in Pickax?

3. Where is Polly from originally?

4. Qwill and Polly share an interest in what?

5. Polly is a widow. What happened to her husband?

6. Polly's father was a Shakespearean scholar. What did he name her? Where did this name come from?

🐾 Qwill's Living Quarters

1. After Qwill decides to turn the mansion into a museum, where do he and the cats move?

2. How many rooms did Qwill have in his carriage-house apartment?

Dining Out

1. With whom does Qwill enjoy the following meal prepared by Mrs. Cobb: sweet potato casserole, Mrs. Cobb's baked ham, ginger-pear salad, and milk chocolate mousse?

2. Whom does Qwill bring to Pickax to manage The Old Stone Mill?

3. What is the name of the new chef at The Old Stone Mill?

4. Who is Antoine Delapierre?

5. Who invents "Fabulous Frozen Foods for Fussy Felines"?

6. Who prepares roast beef and Yorkshire pudding and currant scones for Qwill?

Crimes and Victims

1. How is Senior Goodwinter killed?

2. Amos and Hettie Spence and Mrs. Gage provided Qwill with information about the deaths of Ephraim and Titus Goodwinter. According to them, how did Ephraim and Titus die?

3. How did Gertrude Goodwinter and Harry Noyton die?

4. Who is the arsonist that sets fire to the Klingenschoen Mansion? What happens to him?

5. How does Tony Peters die?

6. Who is responsible for Senior Goodwinter's death? How?

7. What is Herb Hackpole's real name?

THE CAT WHO
SNIFFED GLUE

🐾 General Questions

1. According to Chief Brodie, the most serious problems facing the police in Pickax City are "D_ _ _ _ _ d_ _ _ _ _ _ _! U_ _ _ _ _ _ _ _! d_ _ _ _ _ _ _ _ V_ _ _ _ _ _ _ _ _! That's what runs us ragged!"

2. Whom does Brodie reluctantly reveal as the suspected leader of the hoodlums who might be causing some of the vandalism in Pickax?

3. Who is Winston?

4. What play is the Theatre Club currently rehearsing?

5. Fran plans a surprise birthday party for Qwilleran. How did she know it was his birthday?

6. Bear Paw, Arctic, Michigan, and Beavertail are all examples of what?

7. Who suggests *Moose County Chronicle* or *Clarion* or *Crier* or *Caucus* as possible names for the newspaper?

8. What is the banner headline for the first issue of the *Moose County Something*? What was the story's subheading?

9. What do Mildred's tarot cards reveal about the Fitch murders?

10. What does Fran reveal to Qwill about his 1805 gunboat picture?

11. What is the name of Harley Fitch's boat?

12. After college, Harley spent a year in the east. Where was he and why?

13. Eddington discovers in the rare book collection that a book is missing. Which book is it?

14. Why did Koko take an instant liking to Harley Fitch, Edd Smith, Wally Toddwhistle, and the paperhanger?

15. When the Klingenschoen Theatre opens, it will premiere a revue written by whom?

Chronological Order of Events
Arrange the following events in their order of occurrence.

_____ Qwill accompanies Eddington Smith to the Fitch mansion to dust books.

_____ Koko discovers a secret door in the Fitch library.

_____ Harley Fitch and his wife, Belle, are shot to death in their home.

_____ Qwill is attacked by David Fitch.

_____ Margaret Fitch suffers a stroke.

_____ The *Moose County Something* gets a new name.

_____ Chad Lanspeak and two friends are killed in a car-train collision.

_____ Margaret Fitch dies, and Nigel Fitch commits suicide.

_____ Qwill discovers that his writing studio shows "signs of vandalism."

_____ Qwill plans to visit The Captain's Mess to inquire about his 1805 gunboat picture.

_____ Qwill is run off the road and loses the cats.

_____ Qwill visits the Toddwhistle Taxidermy Studio.

_____ Qwill and Koko visit the Goodwinter Museum, and while there Koko paws at the model ships donated by Harley Fitch.

🐾 Koko and Yum Yum

1. Right after the murder, Koko began to take "a sudden interest in all things nautical." What picture did he tilt? And what books did he begin to sniff?

2. According to Qwill, what genre of books does Koko prefer?

3. Which behaviors/characteristics describe Koko (K) and which ones describe Yum Yum (Y)?

_____ "High-decibel yowl"

_____ The "inspector general"

_____ Screens everyone for security reasons

_____ Fishes cashews out of the bowl and bats them around the room

_____ Licks glue from the flaps of envelopes

_____ "Steals anything small and shiny"

_____ Turns around three times in Qwill's lap before settling down

🐾 Women in Qwill's Life

Who is who? Qwill enjoys the company of Fran Brodie, Polly Duncan, and Mrs. Cobb in The Cat Who Sniffed Glue. _Identify each statement as one that describes Fran (F), Polly (P), or Mrs. Cobb (MC)._

_____ Qwill has never felt entirely comfortable with this woman.

_____ After presenting her with a gift, Qwill feels a "surge of compassion for her."

_____ Qwill likes spending weekends at her "cozy house in the country."

_____ She is "rediscovering love, and her responses are warm and caring."

_____ Her friendship with Qwill is "noticeably cool since he joined the Theatre Club."

_____ She criticizes Qwill because he wants to give up writing a novel.

_____ Her strategy to get Qwill is "all too transparent."

_____ She times her visits to coincide with the cocktail hour.

_____ Qwill notices that she looks "prettier than usual in her pink ruffled blouse."

_____ With her it seems "a dinner invitation was almost obligatory."

🐾 Qwill's Living Quarters

1. Where does Qwill live in this story?

2. Who is helping him decorate the apartment?

3. What color and texture of wall coverings has Fran chosen for Qwill's walls?

4. What print hangs over the sofa?

5. Fran wants to do Qwill's bedroom over. What does she suggest?

6. What is the name of the architect that is doing the design for the new theater?

7. How many people will the new theater seat?

🐾 Dining Out

1. Qwill and Fran enjoy herbed trout with wine sauce here. This restaurant, considered "one of the best restaurants in the county," occupies an old stone mansion and offers an ambience of "soft colors, soft textures, and soft lighting." What is the name of the restaurant?

2. Where does Qwill go to eat the "best hamburgers and homemade pie"?

3. Where is the North Pole Café? What nationality of food does it serve?

4. Who invited Qwill over for pot roast, mashed potatoes, and coconut cake with apricot filling?

5. At this restaurant, the "pickerel tasted like fish . . . [the] steak required chewing . . . [and the] lemon-meringue pie was irresistible." A portrait of its namesake hangs in the dining room. What is the name of the restaurant?

6. How was the sheet cake decorated that guests enjoyed at Qwill's surprise birthday party?

Crimes and Victims

1. How does Mrs. Fitch die?

2. How does Mr. Fitch die?

3. According to the police, who was shot first, Belle or Harley?

4. What happened to Chad Lanspeak?

5. How did Qwill know that it was Harley and not David that committed the crimes?

6. Who plots the embezzlement of bank funds, the murders, and Harley's exchanging identities with his brother?

7. Who staged the vandalism at the dental clinic and why?

THE CAT WHO WENT UNDERGROUND

🐾 General Questions

1. Check the reasons why Qwill decided to spend three months at the log cabin.

   _____ His horoscope suggests that it would be a good time to take a trip.
   _____ Polly is going to be away for the summer.
   _____ Terms of the Klingenschoen will stipulate that he do so.
   _____ The refrigerator in his apartment is out of order.
   _____ Pickax is boring during warm weather.

2. How many features does Qwill agree to write weekly? What is his column called?

3. How much does it cost Qwill to join the Glinko's Fast Track?

4. What is the name of the private community on the lake where people live during the summer?

5. What is Polly's theory about Shakespeare?

6. Qwill believes the Glinko business is a racket. True or False?

7. What color of pickup does Clem drive?

8. "The Fourth of July dawned with the sunshine of a flag-waving holiday. . . ." Qwill "dressed in what he considered appropriate garb" and headed for the parade. Can you match each municipality in Moose County with its float?

   a. Chipmunk b. Sawdust City c. Mooseville d. Pickax e. Brrr

   _____ "A plastic snow scene with papier-mâché igloo and papier-mâché polar bear"

   _____ A "resurrected [version of] a homemade still"

   _____ "A lumbercamp scene on a flatbed truck"

   _____ "A flatbed crowded with sportsmen and outdoor-lovers . . . fishermen . . . boaters . . . golfers . . . and campers"

   _____ "A tableau of grimy miners wearing candles in their hats and carrying pickaxes"

9. What messages did Mrs. Ascott, the clairvoyant from Lockmaster, deliver to Qwill? From whom were these messages?

10. What is the name of Bushy's boat?

11. What happened to Qwill's new addition?

12. What is Iggy's last name?

13. What does Qwill discover about the relationship of Mrs. Wimsey and Little Jo?

14. When Qwill biked out to Hogback Road, whose jacket did he find in the mud near Little Jo's house?

15. Why did Riker break down and buy a horoscope column for the *Moose County Something*?

🐾 Chronological Order of Events
Arrange the following events in their order of occurrence.

   _____ Koko attacks a copy of the *Moose County Something*. He destroys Qwill's column on Emma and her cat, Punkin.

_____ Qwill and the cats drive to the log cabin to spend the summer months.

_____ Little Jo's father, Joe Trupp, is killed when a dump truck tailgate falls on him.

_____ Qwill arrives at the cabin to find a "crumpled rug that is supposed to cover a trapdoor" in the floor.

_____ Qwill hires Clem Cottle to build an addition to the cabin.

_____ Buddy Yarrow slips off the bank, hits his head, and drowns.

_____ Koko destroys "an entire page of the newspaper with the story on page one about the drowning of Buddy Yarrow."

_____ Qwill believes carpenters are "dying and disappearing at an unusual rate."

_____ Qwill reads stories from the notebooks given to him by Emma Wimsey.

_____ A storm hits while Roger, Bushy, and Qwill are on Three Tree Island.

_____ Iggy returns to town and agrees to finish Qwill's addition.

_____ Captain Phlogg dies.

_____ While "digging industriously" under the cabin, Koko discovers the body of Iggy.

_____ Emma's notebooks reveal that Little Jo is her granddaughter.

_____ Qwill, Nick, and Koko find marks on the joist, written in lipstick.

_____ Qwill confronts Little Jo, and she tells him that "Louise" killed the carpenter.

_____ Mrs. Ascott delivers her messages.

Koko and Yum Yum

1. What two columns does Koko shred into pieces?

2. Who is a "lapcat, very affectionate, with all kinds of catly traits," Koko or Yum Yum?

3. Who has "a keen intuition about people, situations, and events," Koko or Yum Yum?

4. Which cat prefers to sit on the moose head, between the antlers?

5. When Lori calls Qwill, who provides "yowls and musical yiks and cadenzas that Lori seem[s] to understand"?

Women in Qwill's Life

1. Where is Polly spending the summer?

2. Why must Polly shorten her visit?

3. Who does Qwill invite to dine with him at the Fish Tank?

4. After dinner, on the way back to the cabin, Qwill reflected on Mildred's "charitable nature and her spunk . . . the firm way she handled the whitefish situation . . . her concern for the lonely girl . . . her initiative . . . and she was a superb cook!" This caused him to realize that he could forgive her for her silliness about what?

Qwill's Living Quarters

1. How old is the Klingenschoen cabin?

2. How far across the water is Canada?

3. Qwill was convinced that the "Glinko network . . . [was] . . . a racket." Can you arrange in their order of occurrence the house repairs that required Qwill to call Glinko Services?

_____ No heat	_____ Water heater problems
_____ Mice in the cabin	_____ Circuit breaker
_____ Plumbing problems	_____ Fireplace and chimney
_____ Fallen trees	problems
_____ Gas smell in the cabin	_____ Water leak

4. What is Qwill's legal address?

Dining Out

1. What is the Fish Tank restaurant in Mooseville, located in "an old waterfront warehouse on the fishing wharves," famous for?

2. What is the name of "the cool place to go for hot cuisine"? What are the specialties there?

3. This restaurant in Lockmaster has a "hostess in long dress, several diners in dinner jackets, and a wine steward." Roger and Qwill dine here on vichyssoise and prime rib. What's the name of the restaurant?

4. At the Wimsey Family Reunion, "long rows of picnic tables were set up, and families arrived with hampers, coolers, and folding lawn chairs. . . . The long tables were loaded with . . ." Can you unscramble the food items enjoyed by members of the Wimsey family?

   Dfier ckenchi   Hemoedam frzreee pklices
   Bkaed bnsea   Lapep jceui aadls
   Hsiocnr ssietap   Nnygar wmysesi lateccooh heest kcae
   Mah sdwiesanch   Bbeerrymthil epi
   Dvldeei esgg   Mosessal cokosei
   Nnreoiu pttoao aadls

5. Whose "casserole . . . sauced with combination of turkey, homemade noodles, and artichoke hearts" puts Qwill "in an excellent frame of mind"?

Crimes and Victims

1. Who is the first carpenter to die? How does he die?

2. What is the name of the underground builder who disappeared while working for the Comptons?

3. What really happened to Captain Phlogg?

4. Can you arrange the order in which the five carpenters were killed?

   _____ Mert   _____ Iggy Small
   _____ Clem Cottle   _____ Buddy Yarrow
   _____ Joe Trupp

5. Why did Louise, alias Little Jo, kill the carpenters?

THE CAT WHO
TALKED TO GHOSTS

🐾 General Questions

1. When Polly returned from England, what opera cassette did she bring to Qwill?

2. From whom did Mrs. Cobb inherit the Goodwinter farmhouse?

3. Who is chairperson of the Goodwinter Farmhouse Museum?

4. What is Mrs. Cobb's son's name?

5. What does Mrs. Cobb's son ask Qwill to look over and "see if anything clicks"?

6. In what year did the explosion in the Goodwinter mine occur?

7. Ephraim Goodwinter's family maintains that his death "was suicide, but the rumor was circulated via the Pickax grapevine that he was lynched." What is the name of the fraternal order whose members claim to be direct descendants of the lynch mob?

8. What is the name of Polly's new kitten?

9. What two items did Mrs. Cobb bequeath to Qwill?

10. When Qwill finally permits Koko to go into the museum ("He had been allowed in the exhibit area once before when Mrs. Cobb was alive"), where does Koko go, and what is he attracted to?

11. Koko "showed no interest in historic documents or the distinguished collection of early lighting devices" in the museum. However, which exhibit seems to fascinate him?

12. How did Kristi Fugtree know that her grandmother was beautiful?

13. What is Kristi's grandmother's name?

14. What are Saanens and Nubians?

15. What book does Kristi give to Qwill?

16. The Goodwinter Museum was planning to unveil a new exhibit. What was the subject of this new exhibit?

17. Fran found a questionable photo with the date October 30, 1904, scribbled on the back. What is it a photo of?

18. Koko's behavior causes Qwill to call Lori Bamba. Lori "seemed to know all about cats." A few minutes prior to Qwill calling Lori, Koko pushes two books off the shelves. What books did he unshelve?

19. What is missing from the new disaster exhibit?

20. What does Mildred discover is missing from the school desk under the telephone?

21. What are the following: Washington, Albion, and Columbian?

22. The story goes that Ephraim's body wasn't in its coffin the day of his funeral. According to an old blacksmith's story, where is his body?

23. What two supposed hoaxes does Adam Dingleberry expose to Qwill?

24. What does Qwill discover in the false bottom of Mrs. Cobb's Dingleberry desk?

25. How much did Lucy Bosworth receive from Titus Goodwinter to compensate for her husband's death?

26. Who took Mrs. Cobb's cookbook?

27. What caused the knocking Mrs. Cobb heard?

🐾 Chronological Order of Events
Arrange the following events in their order of occurrence.

_____ Qwill finds Mrs. Cobb's body at the Goodwinter Museum.

_____ Mrs. Cobb's son reveals that his mother had a heart condition.

_____ Qwill and the cats move to the Goodwinter Farmhouse Museum.

_____ Koko goes to the "exact spot where Mrs. Cobb had collapsed."

_____ Kristi Waffle's goats are poisoned.

_____ Qwilleran unravels the Bosworth family tree.

_____ Police search for Vince Boswell/Bosworth.

_____ Qwill finds "an arched tunnel."

_____ Qwill interviews Adam Dingleberry.

_____ Qwill finds Koko huddled down on a piece of soiled cloth.

_____ Koko and Qwill discover the Halloween box used to frighten Mrs. Cobb.

_____ Vince kills Brent Waffle.

_____ Koko begins knocking books off the shelves.

_____ Koko burrows under the oriental rug.

_____ Qwill returns the incriminating papers to the Dingleberry desk.

🐾 Koko and Yum Yum
1. Which cat is put into a trance by opera?

2. What was Koko's reaction when Vince Boswell referred to him as "kitty"?

3. Tilting pictures, knocking books on the floor, dislodging lamp-shades, and shredding bathroom tissue were examples of how Koko and Yum Yum dealt with what?

4. When Qwill explains to Lori Bamba that "[s]omething is bothering Koko," she suggests that Qwill feed him more _____.

🐾 Women in Qwill's Life
Which is which? Is it Polly (P) or Mildred (M) that is described by the following statements?

_____ She's "intelligent, cultivated, stimulating, loving . . . and jealous."

_____ According to Qwill, she has been "reduced overnight to a blithering fool."

_____ She has an eye for color, design, and coordination.

_____ She is not "attuned to fashion."

_____ She has a new kitten named Bootsie.

_____ She teaches art and home economics.

🐾 Qwill's Living Quarters
1. On what road is the Goodwinter Farmhouse Museum?

2. For how much did Mrs. Cobb sell the Goodwinter farm to the Historical Society?

3. There is a Pennsylvania German *Schrank* in the parlor. Where did Mrs. Cobb get this piece of furniture?

4. Qwill has a nightmare about the "priceless General Grant bed." What is the nightmare?

5. Which statements about the Goodwinter farmhouse are correct? Check all that are correct.

_____ a. The original section of the house was built of "square logs . . . chinked with mortar made of clay, straw, and hog's blood."

_____ b. Originally the basement had a dirt floor.

_____ c. Architectural features of the house include cedar shingles, milled woodwork, six-over-six windows, many with wavy glass, and a barn with a gambrel roof.

_____ d. The east and west wings are the oldest parts of the farm-house.

_____ e. There is an eye of the needle cut into the larger barn door.

🐾 Dining Out

1. Qwill invites Mildred to dinner. "I'll pick you up at six-thirty, and we'll go to the Northern Lights Hotel." Unscramble what Mildred and Qwill select:

   Bldoier ihwteshfi   Grfo gles

   Pttiee dlsaa   Ppmnkiu ecnap iep

   Fnrehc oonni puos

2. This is the place where "serious eaters" converge. It started in a small log cabin in the 1930s and is located in North Kennebeck. What is the name of the restaurant?

3. What nationality of food that Polly is cooking causes Qwill to remark that she is "whipping a good idea to death"?

4. Where does Qwill find "old-fashioned bread pudding with a pitcher of thick cream" and coffee "powerful enough to exorcise demons and domesticate poltergeists"?

🐾 Crimes and Victims

1. Who killed Mrs. Cobb?

2. How was Mrs. Cobb killed?

3. Who killed Kristi's goats?

4. Who killed Brent Waffle and how?

CHARACTER
IDENTIFICATION II

Who is who? Can you identify the following characters?

1. He is a photographer and has a photo studio in Lockmaster. He is an avid fisherman.

2. She and her baby live with Vince. Actually, though, she isn't Vince's wife. What is her real name?

3. She is an assistant in Amanda Goodwinter's interior design studio. She also directed the Theatre Club's production of *Arsenic and Old Lace*.

4. This twenty-nine-year-old carpenter from Mooseville drowned while fishing, apparently after slipping down the riverbank and hitting his head on a rock.

5. She's "real old but still sharp" and has a "wonderful cat story" that she shares with Qwill. We also learn that she is Little Jo's grandmother.

6. He is the owner of the bar at Hotel Booze. He is a "hefty man with a sailor's tan . . . black hair, and a bushy black beard."

7. Qwill's English teacher who regularly assigned "a thousand words on such subjects as the weather, breakfast, or the color green."

8. A "popular lawman . . . an amiable Scot . . ." who is the police chief and Francesca's father.

9. The superintendent of Pickax schools.

10. Oldest mortician in three counties.

11. Qwill's gardener in Pickax. He also writes a gardening column for the *Moose County Something*.

12. Waitress at the Black Bear Café in the Hotel Booze in Brrr. She serves hamburgers "with her thumb on the top of the bun to hold it all together."

13. Taxidermist in Pickax. He builds sets for the Theatre Club.

14. A forty-three-year-old carpenter who is killed when the tailgate of his truck falls on him.

15. He killed Titus Goodwinter in a fight.

16. Owner of Edd's Editions in Pickax.

17. Young woman who is spending the summer at the Dunfield House in Mooseville. She dresses like she is in the 1930s, and she likes to walk on the beach.

18. Owner of Scottie's Men's Store and chief of the vounteer fire department.

19. He invents a line of frozen gourmet meals for cats called "Fabulous Foods for Fussy Felines."

20. A "school janitor for forty years" and now Qwill's houseman at the mansion in Pickax.

21. A "self-made man with a talent for attracting women as well as money" who dies in an accident with Gritty Goodwinter when their car collides with a buck deer.

22. Night desk clerk at the New Pickax Hotel. A good-looking young man who applies for the job of manager at the Goodwinter Farmhouse Museum.

23. Polly's landlord in Moose County. After Polly's husband was killed, this man offered Polly the cottage rent-free.

24. Owner of the Lanspeak Department Store in Pickax. He and his wife are the "life blood of the Theatre Club."

25. A clean-cut young man, the son of Iris Cobb, he plans to open a construction business in Moose County.

CLUES, CLUES, CLUES II

Can you identify the mystery based on the list of clues provided?

1. Tilted picture of an 1805 gunboat
   Captains Courageous
   Two Years Before the Mast
   Mutiny on the Bounty
   Moby-Dick
   Twins
   A taxidermist, a paperhanger, and a book binder

   _____

2. Goodwinter Farmhouse Museum
   Bed pillow
   Oriental rugs
   Family Bible
   Escape tunnel
   To Kill a Mockingbird
   One Flew Over the Cuckoo's Nest

   _____

3. Crumpled rug over trapdoor
   Tap, tap, tap
   Lipstick marks on floor joist
   Emma Wimsey and Punkin
   Carpenters

   _____

4. Graffiti
   Junk jewelry
   Daisies
   "Three Blind Mice"
   Bike accident
   Initials: S. G.

   _____

5. Iron herb garden
   Smashed clay pot
   Arson
   Old plank bridge
   Hamlet
   Macbeth
   Julius Caesar
   A Midsummer Night's Dream

   _____

PLACES, PLACES, PLACES II

How many places do you remember from your reading? See how many you can identify.

1. Café located in Hotel Booze in Brrr where you can get delicious pies.

2. Dentist office in Pickax.

3. This company, the second largest contractor in Moose County, developed the Indian Village apartments and condominiums.

4. Café in Brrr with one restroom that is "not to be believed."

5. The presidential suite in this hotel is the only one with a telephone and color TV.

6. This group is helping to operate the Klingenschoen Museum and also oversees the Goodwinter Farmhouse Museum.

7. The largest commercial building on Main Street.

8. Complex of apartments and condominiums on Ittibittiwassee River.

9. Law firm that handles the Klingenschoen fund and Mrs. Cobb's inheritance.

10. The "oldest flophouse in the county" whose dim lighting in the dining room "camouflages the dreary walls, ancient linoleum floor, and worn plastic tables."

11. Bookstore in Pickax that has a "smell of old books and sardines."

12. Pickax funeral home that makes the arrangements for Iris Cobb's funeral.

13. This area has been a ghost town for fifty years. It's located about thirty minutes from Pickax. The Goodwinter Farmhouse Museum is here.

14. This is the creek that runs across the back of the Goodwinter and Fugtree properties.

15. This village is on the lake and the coldest spot in Moose County.

16. This is the "slummiest town in the county." It is also known as the "moonshine capital of the county."

17. This town is northeast of Pickax.

18. This town has an "air of sophistication" lacking in Moose County and is sixty miles southwest of Mooseville.

19. The point on the lake at Mooseville where the big salmon bite.

20. This town used to be the center of the lumbering industry.

QWILL QUIZ II

What new things have you learned about Qwill? Take the quiz and find out.

1. Where do Qwill's ties come from?

2. What color are all of Qwill's ties?

3. Whom does Qwill hire as his secretary?

4. "Like that of every other Moose County adult," what is Qwill's chief concern now?

5. Qwill decides to write a history of the *Pickax Picayune*. True or False?

6. Who encourages Qwill to write an "original revue" for the grand opening of the new playhouse?

7. Who is Qwill's first featured person in his column for the *Moose County Something*?

8. What is Qwill's column called?

9. What had Qwill never done until he moved to the Goodwinter farmhouse?

10. What is the first thing Qwill does when he returns home?

THE GOODS ON
THE GOODWINTERS

How much do you really know about the Goodwinters? Answer as many questions as you can about one or another of the Goodwinter family members.

1. Junior's father is _____ and his father is _____ and his father is _____.

2. Melinda's father is _____.

3. What is Junior's brother's name? Where does he live?

4. What is Junior's sister's name? Where does she live?

5. Ephraim had two sons. Who are they, and which one is the oldest?

6. Melinda and her brother "grew up like twins." What is Melinda's brother's name?

7. Which two Goodwinters served as Aunt Fanny's attorneys?

8. Which Goodwinter founded the *Pickax Picayune*?

9. A "gray-haired woman with a perpetual scowl . . ." this Goodwinter is one of the "Drinking Goodwinters." Who is she?

10. To whom is Jody Goodwinter married?

11. This Goodwinter seduced Ellie Whittlestaff. He is also Senior's father. Who is he?

12. This Goodwinter has "attractive green eyes and the longest eyelashes" Qwill has ever seen. "She never really wanted to be a country doctor" but she "was hot to marry Qwill." Who is she?

13. What is Gertrude "Gritty" Goodwinter's maiden name?

14. Match the Goodwinter with his/her occupation.

a. Interior decorator   _____ Penelope Goodwinter
b. Attorney   _____ Melinda Goodwinter
c. Doctor   _____ Amanda Goodwinter
d. Lumber baron   _____ Hal Goodwinter
e. Dental hygienist   _____ Ephraim Goodwinter
f. Founder of the *Pickax Picayune*   _____ Jody Goodwinter

15. Unfortunately, many of the Goodwinters met with untimely deaths. Match each to his/her manner of death.

a. Killed with a knife.
b. Car strikes Old Stone Bridge.
c. Crashes car into monument at end of Goodwinter Boulevard.
d. Commits suicide.
e. Supposedly his horse was frightened.
f. Hanged himself. Some believe he was lynched.
g. Car crash with Harry Noyton.
h. Dies after a lengthy illness.

_____ Dr. Melinda Goodwinter
_____ Mrs. Hal Goodwinter
_____ Samson Goodwinter
_____ Senior Goodwinter
_____ Titus Goodwinter
_____ Penelope Goodwinter
_____ Gertrude "Gritty" Gage Goodwinter
_____ Ephraim Goodwinter

READ ALL ABOUT IT! NEWSPAPERS "400 MILES NORTH OF EVERYWHERE"

Can you identify which statements below describe each of the newspapers read by residents "400 miles north of everywhere"?

(DF) *Daily Fluxion*
(PP) *Pickax Picayune*
(MCS) *Moose County Something*

(MR) *Morning Rampage*
(LL) *Lockmaster Logger*
(SG) *Spudsboro Gazette*

_____ Similar to the *Moose County Something*, with circulation in the Potato Mountains.

_____ Circulation of 427,463.

_____ The publisher's slogan is *Fiat Flux*.

_____ Founded in 1859.

_____ Residents over ninety receive a free subscription.

_____ Circulation is 11,500.

_____ Its editor is Kipling MacDiarmid.

_____ Owned by Pennimans and in competition with the _Daily Flux-ion._

_____ Noted for its "twenty-four-point bylines and meager wage scale."

_____ This paper has a "slick, color-coordinated, acoustically engineered, electronically equipped workstation environment."

_____ Originally housed in a rented warehouse, a former meat-packing facility.

_____ Its slogan is "Read all about it."

_____ Originally published twice a week but now expanded to five days a week.

_____ Its new building was made possible by an interest-free loan from the K fund.

_____ Senior Goodwinter hand-sets most of the type.

_____ A modest run of thirty-two hundred copies for each issue was normal.

_____ This paper covers all the ice cream socials and chicken dinners.

THE CAT WHO
LIVED HIGH

🐾 General Questions

1. What does SOCK stand for?

2. When Polly calls Qwill to tell him that she is being evicted from her house in the country, where does Qwill suggest that she move?

3. What color is Qwill's new car?

4. What is Qwill's apartment number at the Casablanca?

5. Who lives in 14B?

6. What does Qwill discover under the base of the bar where Koko has been sniffing?

7. Who was the tenant in Qwill's apartment before he moved in? What happened to this person?

8. What happened to Gus, the doorman at the Casablanca?

9. What is the name of the new proposed building that would span Zwinger Boulevard and have two towers?

10. What was the name of the firm promoting the new building project?

11. What was the number of Qwill's parking spot?

12. According to Mary, "The countess has one interest in life." What is it?

13. When Qwill determines that someone has been feeding the cats, in the process, what does he notice is missing?

14. Koko leads Qwill to find a gold bracelet between the seat cushions of the library sofa. What initials were engraved on two of the discs in the bracelet?

15. Besides the initials engraved on two of the discs, what was engraved on the remaining discs?

16. How many ways was Bessinger's first name spelled in archived news clips that Qwill found at the *Daily Fluxion*? What were they?

17. The Bessinger-Todd Gallery had the same address as the Lambreth Gallery. True or False?

18. What memorial does Qwill propose to honor Ms. Bessinger?

19. Who does the countess name as heir to the Casablanca?

20. What four words did Qwill make from the Scrabble tiles that Koko had dislodged: H, O, R, S, B, X, and A?

21. Who is assigned parking space #27? What space was he assigned previously?

22. What does the Klingenschoen board vote to do regarding Qwill's proposition to save the Casablanca?

23. How does Qwill deduce that Ross couldn't be the killer?

24. Who is Randy Jupiter?

25. What was Dianne Bessinger's cat's name?

26. With what does Jupiter attack Qwill?

27. Who does Qwill suspect planted dynamite between the twelfth and fourteenth floors?

28. Qwill suspects that Jupiter and Dunwoody were agents for Fleudd. True or False?

🐾 Chronological Order of Events
Arrange the events in their order of occurrence.

_____ Qwill learns that the former tenant of the apartment, Dianne Bessinger, was murdered in the apartment.

_____ Koko curls his tail in "corkscrew" fashion.

_____ Koko and Qwill again play Scrabble, and this time the word JOVE appears.

_____ Koko leads Qwill to the library sofa, where Qwill finds a gold bracelet between the seat cushions.

_____ An explosion rocks Casablanca.

_____ Qwill believes that Ross was framed.

_____ Qwill and the cats move into the Casablanca.

_____ Qwill smashes a bottle on Jupiter's head.

_____ Qwill discovers that Dunwoody, an expert with explosives, and Jupiter were agents for Fleudd.

_____ Koko is attracted to an eight-foot bar in the middle of the floor of the sunken living room.

_____ Qwill realizes that someone planted a bomb, which destroyed the top floors of the Casablanca.

_____ Koko moves the bloody butcher block painting in the apartment.

_____ Qwill realizes that Ross didn't write the message on the wall.

_____ Qwill moves the bar and uncovers a large, dark bloodstain.

_____ Qwill confronts Randy Jupiter, and Jupiter pulls a knife on Qwill.

_____ Qwill takes the picture down from the wall and with the assistance of a lamp, he is able to read faint letters covered with fresh paint: FORGIVE ME DIANE.

_____ Qwill puts the words AGENT, HOAX, and JOVE together and arrives at what he thinks is the solution to the murder.

_____ Koko wakes Qwill in the middle of the night. Qwill hears a "rustling, crackling, creaking" under the floor. He immediately sounds an alarm.

🐾 Koko and Yum Yum

1. Which cat likes the "sensation of the waterbed"?

2. Crumpled paper is "like catnip" to which cat?

3. What flavors of ice cream do the cats *not* like?

4. How do Koko and Yum Yum react when they learn they are moving to the Casablanca for the winter?

🐾 Women in Qwill's Life
Who is who?

1. While living at the Casablanca, whom does Qwill call "Madame Defarge?"

2. Who is an officer in SOCK and is "preppy [with] pearls and everything"?

3. To whom does Qwill find it difficult to "reveal his true feelings because he's tongue-tied"?

4. Since his last meeting with her, "her strikingly-brunette hair was a different color . . . and style—lighter, redder, and frizzier. She now does "clerical work" at an auction house. Who is she?

5. She is a resident at the Casablanca. She drives a BMW and has a "model's walk and an heiress's clothing budget." Who is she?

🐾 Qwill's Living Quarters

1. In what year was the Casablanca built?

2. In what city is the Casablanca?

3. What color is the exterior of the building?

4. What does the building resemble?

5. On what floor does the countess live?

6. How many elevators are there in the Casablanca?

🐾 Dining Out

Match the menu to the occasion.

a. Antipasti, "breaded baby squid with marinara sauce, and roasted red peppers with anchovies and onion"; soup, a "rich chicken broth threaded with egg and cheese"; a "rib chop with wine and mushroom sauce"; a bottle of Valpolicella; a "medium-priced *vitello alla piccata*, sautéed with lemon and capers"; and for dessert, "gelato and espresso."

b. "The soup course was cream of watercress, followed by crabcakes with shiitake mushrooms, baby beets in an orange glaze, and wild rice. A salad of artichoke hearts and sprouts was served . . . and the meal ended with a chocolate soufflé."

c. French onion soup with roast beef sandwiches with horseradish.

d. "The entrée was shrimp Newburgh, preceded by a slice of pâté and followed by . . . Waldorf salad." The meal concluded with "bananas Foster."

_____ Qwill and Amberina eat at Roberto's.
_____ Qwill and Matt Thiggamon at the Press Club.
_____ Qwill and the countess at the Casablanca.
_____ Qwill, Courtney, and Amberina at Courtney's.

🐾 Crimes and Victims

1. How did Dianne Bessinger die?

2. How did Ross Rasmus die?

3. Who planted the dynamite at the Casablanca? What happens to this person?

4. Who was the apparent mastermind of the murder and the explosion? Who assisted him?

THE CAT WHO KNEW A CARDINAL

🐾 General Questions

1. Qwill now lives in the apple barn. Who designed and engineered the renovation?

2. What was Hilary VanBrook called behind his back?

3. Who played Queen Katharine? Where is she from?

4. Which play did the Theatre Club perform?

5. Why does Wally Toddwhistle's mother think that he'll be a suspect in the death of Hilary VanBrook?

6. Whose idea was it to have a "Tipsy Look-Alike Contest"?

7. Who is the panel of judges for the "Tipsy Look-Alike Contest"?

8. What is Qwill's new hobby that also provides Koko with a pastime?

9. Several people begin to inquire about Dennis Hough. What is Qwill's response to their inquiries?

10. Who spots Dennis Hough's van and follows it to the cabin on Qwill's property?

11. What is the message that Hough's wife left for him on his answering machine?

12. "Died suddenly" is the euphemism in the north country for _____.

13. How much money did VanBrook request for Fiona's travel expenses? How much did he actually pay her?

14. How much is the reward offered for information regarding VanBrook's shooting?

15. What was the name of the horse that Robbie Stucker would ride?

16. Who owned the horse Stucker would ride?

17. What is the name of the newsletter that is a collection of steeplechase news?

18. Ultra Bodoni and Eramus are types of what?

19. Who trained Robbie's horse?

20. What was the early connection between Fiona and VanBrook?

21. VanBrook promised to put Robbie through college if he would study what?

22. What does Mildred think the "sprig of green leaves with a purple flower" that Qwill put in his pocket might be?

23. To whom does VanBrook leave his entire estate?

24. What did Qwill find interleafed in several books he brought home for VanBrook's collection?

25. Apparently, the red dot on boxes signified what?

26. Who finds a copy of Qwill's book, *City of Brotherly Crime*?

27. What happens to O'Hare when confronted by Qwill?

28. What clues does Qwill use to explain to Polly why he was certain that the killer was Steve O'Hare?

🐾 Chronological Order of Events

Arrange the following events in their order of occurrence.

_____ During the cast party, Koko sits on the *Schrank* and stares at the top of VanBrook's head.

_____ Dennis Hough disappears without a clue.

_____ Koko strikes up an acquaintance with a cardinal.

_____ Edd Smith finds a copy of Qwill's book, *City of Brotherly Crime*, and brings it to Qwill.

_____ Qwill invites Steve O'Hare to visit. When he arrives, Qwill asks Edd to "stay there and listen, out of sight."

_____ Hixie Rice tells Qwill that she saw Hough's van turn into the K property.

_____ Koko scatters red jelly beans and shreds the *Stablechat* newsletter.

_____ Qwill finds a message from Dennis Hough's wife, telling him never to come home and that she wants a divorce.

_____ After the cast party at the barn, Qwill finds a car in the orchard and the driver slumped over the wheel, shot in the back of the head.

_____ Qwill returns home and finds the body of Dennis Hough hanging from an overhead beam.

_____ Steve O'Hare shoots Koko's cardinal.

_____ In VanBrook's library, Qwill finds a catalog of all the books.

_____ Qwill discovers papers and old documents belonging to VanBrook in a hollow volume, *Memoirs of a Merry Milkmaid*.

_____ Koko knocks books Qwill brought from VanBrook's to the floor, and Qwill discovers that they are interleafed with counterfeit money.

_____ Qwill confronts Steve, and when Steve pulls a gun, the apple tree hanging falls on him.

_____ Qwill hits O'Hare with a frozen rabbit.

🐾 Koko and Yum Yum

1. Whose law is "If anything can be unhooked, untied, unbuckled, or unlatched, DO IT!"?

2. When Bushy comes to photograph the house for insurance purposes, how does the behavior of Koko and Yum Yum differ from when they were in his studio?

3. How do the cats react to Qwill's attempt at entertaining them with the bubble pipe?

🐾 Women in Qwill's Life
Which is which? In The Cat Who Knew a Cardinal, _Polly, Mildred Hanstable, and Susan Exbridge vie for Qwill's attention. For each statement below, identify which lady—Polly (P), Mildred (M), or Susan (S)—is described._

_____ She has become disinterested.
_____ She recently became a widow.
_____ She is one of Qwill's favorite cooks.
_____ Qwill and this lady have been "close friends" for two years.
_____ She is "too aggressive and too theatrical" for Qwill.
_____ She's "never . . . read a book."
_____ She begins wearing brighter colors.
_____ She and Qwill consult "on every question."
_____ She is "more fashionable" than the rest.

🐾 Qwill's Living Quarters

1. Who was the original builder of the apple barn in which Qwill now lives?

2. When was the barn originally built?

3. On warm days there is still an aroma of Winesaps and Jonathans in the barn. True or False?

4. How many levels of balconies are there in the barn?

5. What is in the center of the apple barn?

6. On which balcony is Qwill's bedroom and writing studio?

7. On which balcony is the guest room?

8. On which balcony is the cat's apartment?

9. Qwill chose two tapestries to decorate the barn. Where does each one hang?

   a. On the fireplace, facing the foyer
   b. On the railing of the highest catwalk

   _____ A "stylized tree dotted with a dozen bright red apples the size of basketballs"

   _____ A "galaxy of birds and green foliage"

🐾 Dining Out

1. When Polly and Qwill dine out, what is her usual drink?

2. Where is the menu always "steak or fish, take it or leave it"?

3. Where is the crab Louis salad the "genuine thing," according to Qwill?

4. Who prefers his Bloody Mary "extra hot" with "two stalks of celery, and no vodka"?

🐾 Crimes and Victims

1. Who killed VanBrook?

2. Why did Dennis Hough commit suicide?

THE CAT WHO
MOVED A
MOUNTAIN

🐾 General Questions

1. On which side of the Potato Mountains is Big Potato Mountain and Little Potato Mountain?

2. What is the name of the river on the Potato Mountains?

3. How much was the owner of Tiptop asking for the property?

4. Who is Bill Treacle?

5. What is Vonda Dudley Wix's column in the *Spudsboro Gazette* called?

6. Who calls the architecture style of the Tiptop "Musty Rustic"?

7. In the Potato Mountains, you drive "south in order to go north, and down in order to go up." True or False?

8. What does Qwill ask Mr. Beechum to build among the trees?

9. Which is which? Taters (T) or New Taters (NT)?

_____ Ones "whose ancestors bought cheap land from the government . . . and still cling to a pioneer way of life"

_____ Ones who "are the artists and others who deserted the cities for what they call plain living"

10. Potato Cove was once a ghost town. True or False?

11. How old was J. J. Hawkinfield when he died?

12. Where is Mrs. Hawkinfield?

13. For whom does Qwill buy cap jackets? How much does he pay for each jacket?

14. Who had Amy, owner of Amy's Lunch Bucket, planned to marry?

15. What happened to the three Hawkinfield boys?

16. Why does Mrs. Beechum not speak?

17. Qwill sees a revolving circle of light on Little Potato. What is it?

18. Was Forest granted a change of venue?

19. Who tries to tell Beechum's attorney that neither car at the Hawkinfields' house the day of the murder was the Beechum jalopy?

20. Why did Hawkinfield send Sherry to a boarding school?

21. What excuse does Qwill use to interview people he suspects might know something about the Hawkinfield murder?

22. What is the Hot Potato Fund?

23. Why does Qwill suspect that Hawkinfield's daughter had something to do with her father's murder?

24. Qwill tells Sherry that he is a writer of textbooks. What type of textbooks does he tell her he writes?

25. Which clue "hidden under a piece of furniture for a year" does Qwill produce that causes Lumpton to attack him?

26. According to Qwill, which role do Josh, Hugh, and Sherry play in the murder of Hawkinfield?

Chronological Order of Events

Arrange the following events in their order of occurrence.

_____ Koko keeps an eye on Sherry until Sheriff Wilbranks arrives.

_____ Sherry Hawkinfield arrives at Tiptop.

_____ Qwill decides that Hugh killed J.J. in order to protect himself and his father, Josh, who was "the organizer of the bootleg operation."

_____ Qwill discovers a door behind the bookcase.

_____ Qwill finds "an old-fashioned black iron key" hanging behind the picture.

_____ Koko convinces Qwill to open the middle drawer of the desk.

_____ Koko tilts a picture of mountains painted by Forest.

_____ Qwill rents Tiptop, a home on the top of Big Potato Mountain.

_____ Hugh Lumpton grabs the Queen Anne chair and attempts to hit Qwill.

_____ In an unpublished editorial, written by Hawkinfield, Qwill learns about the "Hot Potato Fund."

_____ Qwill grabs the candelabrum and rams it "into his attacker's midriff."

_____ Qwill meets Chrysalis Beechum, sister of Forest Beechum, who is accused of killing J. J. Hawkinfield.

_____ Hugh Lumpton is the court-appointed attorney selected to represent Forest Beechum.

_____ Koko sniffs the bottle of sherry that Qwill brings home. He assumes that Koko is attracted to the smell of the glue on the label.

_____ Qwill places the harness on Koko and walks him around the veranda. Koko "prance[s] in circles with distasteful stares at the edge of the veranda."

_____ Qwill accuses Hugh Lumpton of murdering Hawkinfield.

Koko and Yum Yum

1. In *The Cat Who Moved a Mountain*, neither Koko (K) nor Yum Yum (Y) is anxious to spend the summer in the Potato Mountains. Where does each cat hide?

   _____ Who hides on a bookshelf behind the biographies?

   _____ Who "huddled on a beam under the roof, accessible only by a forty-foot ladder"?

2. How does Qwill finally manage to get the cats to cooperate and hop into the carrier?

3. Someone plans to steal the cats, or so it appears. How does Koko foil this attempt?

4. Which cat enjoys running up and down the staircase at Tiptop?

5. Which painting has Koko taken a liking to this time?

6. Who manages to turn the radio on?

7. Qwill wakes one morning at Tiptop to what he thinks are gunshots. What does he discover the noise really is?

Women in Qwill's Life

1. Who is returning to Pickax to take over her father's medical practice?

2. When Qwill feels the need to converse with someone back home, whom does he call?

3. Who was J. J. Hawkinfield's girlfriend, and what did he call her?

4. While in the Potato Mountains, Qwill interacts with several other women. Match the name to the statement describing her.

   a. Dolly Lessmore   b. Chrysalis Beechum   c. Vonda Dudley Wix
   d. Sherry Hawkinfield   e. Sabrina Peel

_____ She dresses in smart suits and has "the same reddish blond hair" as Fran Brodie.

_____ A columnist for the *Spudsboro Gazette*.

_____ Qwill's real estate agent. She is "on the young side of middle age."

_____ A "tall young woman with hollow cheeks and long, straight hair hanging to her waist." She is a weaver on Little Potato Mountain.

_____ She was once married to Hugh Lumpton. She owns a shop called Not New But Nice.

🐾 Qwill's Living Quarters

1. What does Qwill call the painting of the mountains by Forest Beechum?

2. When was Tiptop Inn built?

3. How many bathrooms are there in Tiptop?

4. According to Sabrina Peel, what was Mrs. Hawkinfield's favorite color?

5. How much is the weekly rent Qwill pays for Tiptop?

6. What is the name of the drive Qwill takes to reach Tiptop?

🐾 Dining Out

1. Match the meal to the restaurant.

   a. Lunch Bucket   b. Pasta Perfect
   c. Five Points Café   d. Spudsboro Golf Club

   _____ Poached flounder "lightly sauced . . . with three perfect green beans, a sliver of parboiled carrot . . . a cherry tomato broiled and sprinkled with parsley."

   _____ A Father's Day Special—"a turkey dinner with cornbread dressing, cranberry sauce, and nips."

   _____ As an appetizer Qwill orders "smoked salmon and avocado rolled in lasagna noodles, with a sauce of watercress, dill and horseradish." For his entrée, he orders "tagliatelle in a sauce of ricotta, leeks and ham."

_____ Vegetable soup "thick with vegetables, including turnips," and a veggieburger.

2. Who brought Qwill some of her "Chocolate Whoppers to boost . . . [his] morale"?

3. In the nonsmoking room of the Pasta Perfect restaurant there is a "painted portait of an Indian chief smoking a peace pipe." True or False?

🐾 Crimes and Victims

1. How is J. J. Hawkinfield killed?

2. Who killed J. J. Hawkinfield? Why?

3. Who collaborated with Hawkinfield's killer?

4. How does Qwill protect himself from the killer?

THE CAT WHO WASN'T THERE

🐾 General Questions

1. How many residents of Moose County travel to Scotland?

2. What does Polly remember about the man following her?

3. Where was the car from that followed Polly?

4. What is the superstition associated with the staging of *Macbeth*?

5. What was the prevailing story about Irma Hasselrich?

6. When Brodie's office ran a check on the maroon car with a Massachusetts license, to whom did the car belong?

7. Mildred decides to do a reading of tarot cards with Qwill present. She has already revealed that the cards suggest a person is in danger: "A mature woman." What does her second reading with Qwill reveal?

8. Who first suspects that Irma and the bus driver are carrying on?

9. What is the room number of Polly and Irma?

10. On what day of the trip does Irma die?

11. Who offers to fly back to the United States with Irma's body?

12. When Qwill calls Mildred back in Pickax to tell her about Irma's death, what unusual thing does Mildred tell Qwill Koko did the night before?

13. Who is accused of stealing Grace Utley's jewelry?

14. How does Qwill find out that Irma knew Bruce and was trying to help him?

15. When Qwill returns home, he asks Mildred if the cats misbehaved in any way. What does she tell him?

16. Which card from Mildred's tarot deck did Koko steal?

17. How does Qwill learn the identity of Katie?

18. What did Koko do to Irma's obituary?

19. Who suggested that Irma's wishes were to be cremated? In actuality, what happened to Irma's body?

20. To whom does Yum Yum give an emery board?

21. What does Qwill suggest about Irma that upsets Polly?

22. What does Mr. Hornbuckle tell Qwill that causes him to suspect that Dr. Hal's son is still alive?

23. When Qwill meets Charles Edward Martin at the Goodwinter house and indicates that they've met before, who does Qwill accuse Martin of being?

24. Melinda visits Qwill and causes him to question her motive for visiting. What does Koko present her with as a parting gift?

25. When Qwill and Nick Bamba find the bearded man in his travel trailer in Shantytown, how does Qwill know that Yum Yum is somewhere in the trailer?

26. Qwill begins to suspect that Charles Edward Martin was, in fact, Emory Goodwinter when Mildred's emery boards are stolen and the payments continue after Emory's supposed death. However, what was the final clue that made Qwill certain he had his man?

27. What does Polly's sister-in-law, who worked for Dr. Melinda, discover about Irma's folder?

28. How does Melinda confess to the murder?

29. What happens to the suicide note that Melinda wrote for Qwill?

Chronological Order of Events
Arrange the following events in their order of occurrence.

_____ Mildred Hanstable reads the tarot cards and warns Qwill about some sort of fraud or treachery.

_____ When Qwill learns that Polly has been followed by a man with a beard, he quickly leaves the Potato Mountains and returns to Pickax.

_____ Koko does "a slow prance around" the half-page obituary of Irma Hasselrich in the *Moose County Something*.

_____ Qwill notices a "youngish man with a bushy beard" driving a maroon car with a Massachusetts license plate.

_____ Qwill returns to the apple barn and finds Koko "in the throes of a catfit."

_____ When Nick and Lori Bamba visit, Yum Yum gives Nick an emery board.

_____ Qwill can't find Yum Yum. He yells, "Treat!" but she doesn't come.

_____ While watching *Macbeth*, Qwill gets that tingling sensation in his moustache. He leaves the theater and hurries home to discover that someone has broken into the house.

_____ Mr. Hornbuckle tells Qwill that Dr. Hal sent his son, Emory, away and "paid 'im money reg'lar iffen he di'n't come back."

_____ Bushy brings his photos from Scotland over to Qwill's house. Koko deglosses three photos of Melinda Goodwinter.

_____ Nick believes that the bearded man, Charles Edward Martin, lives in Shantytown.

_____ Irma Hasselrich dies in her room.

_____ Bruce, the minibus driver, disappears.

_____ Qwill's radio/cassette player, his tapes from his trip to Scotland, and interview tapes are missing.

_____ Qwill and Nick find the bearded man in a trailer in Shantytown.

_____ Qwill yells, "Treat!" and this time Yum Yum responds. In the trailer, in a toilet, "Yum Yum was perched precariously on the rim."

_____ The police pick up Bruce Gow in London. He admits to stealing the jewelry but not to murdering Irma Hasselrich.

_____ Qwilleran realizes that the Boulevard Prowler is Dr. Hal's son, Emory.

_____ Qwill is certain that Emory had a partner. The obvious one is Melinda.

_____ Emory admits that Melinda's plan was to "get rid of Mrs. Duncan."

_____ "Yum Yum's cache of emery boards" causes Qwill to suspect Emory.

_____ Melinda Goodwinter crashes her car into the Goodwinter monument at the end of the street.

_____ Qwill's theory is that Melinda "tampered with some vitamin capsules that Polly had taken to Scotland, substituting a drug that would stop the heart . . . and [i]nadvertently . . . killed one of her best friends."

_____ Koko shreds Melinda's note to Qwill.

Koko and Yum Yum

1. How does Koko suggest to Qwill that Mildred would be a suitable sitter while Qwill is in Scotland?

2. Which cat likes to help Mildred read tarot cards?

3. After melted butter accidentally squirts on the lapel of Qwill's new suede jacket, when he finds his jacket later, what has happened to the butter stain?

4. When Qwill returns home and finds "a pair of debilitated" cats on the rug, he immediately calls Lori Bamba to ask her what she thinks is wrong with them. What does she suggest?

5. Besides licking photos of Melinda and shredding the obituary of Irma, how does Koko suggest to Qwill that he should consider the "pink pills"?

🐾 Women in Qwill's Life
Is it Polly (P) or Melinda (M) that . . .

_____ causes Qwill to return to Moose County "at a speed that discommoded the yowling passengers in the backseat"

_____ makes Qwill "unsure how to handle their reunion"

_____ asks Qwill to marry her for three years, and then he can have his freedom

_____ "is still carrying the torch for him"

_____ causes Qwill to suspect "that the strange look in her eyes was insanity"

_____ was offended when Qwill suggested that Irma was a drug smuggler

_____ Qwill engages in a "warm, silent, meaningful embrace"

_____ Qwill offers a "fervent and lingering handclasp . . . as [an] amorous . . . greeting"

🐾 Dining Out
Match the menu to the restaurant.

a. "Raw vegetables with bagna cauda . . . *zuppi di fagioli* . . . *tortellini quattro formaggi* . . . [*zuccotto*] a concoction of cream, chocolate, and nuts."

b. Samosas, mulligatawny soup, tandoori murghi and pulao, and a side of dal.

c. Thursday's special: "TOM SOUP, TUNA SAMICH and MAC/CHEEZ."

d. Here the specials include: "lovely roasted quail with goat cheese, sun-dried tomatoes, and hickory-smoked bacon. . . ." Other items include grilled swordfish, fillet of beef, and a dessert that is "a delicate terrine of three kinds of chocolate drenched in raspberry coulis."

e. "Haggis, tatties and neeps, Forfar bridies, Pitlochry salad, tea, short-bread, and a 'wee dram' for toasting."

f. New selections here include: "French onion soup . . . grilled salmon steak . . . chicken cordon bleu . . . and roast prime rib. . . ." The chef, however, doesn't know the difference between chicken Kiev and chicken cordon bleu.

_____ An Indian restaurant in Glasgow, Scotland
_____ The New Pickax Hotel
_____ The Dimsdale Diner
_____ The Palomino Paddock
_____ Linguini's
_____ Scottish Night at the Lodge Hall

Crimes and Victims

1. Was Melinda and Emory's plot to murder Polly or hold her for ransom?

2. Who killed Irma Hasselrich?

3. How does Qwill think Melinda killed Irma?

4. Why did Melinda commit suicide?

5. Did the bus driver, Bruce, admit to stealing the jewelry?

6. Charles Edward Martin was charged with breaking and entering, loitering, and shoplifting. True or False?

THE CAT WHO
WENT INTO THE
CLOSET

🐾 General Questions

1. Who wrote and performed the docudrama *The Big Burning of 1869*?

2. Who produced and directed *The Big Burning of 1869*?

3. In *The Cat Who Went Into the Closet*, which character likes to throw around French phrases?

4. Where did Qwill get the information he needed in order to write the documentary about the fire of 1869?

5. According to Euphonia Gage, what color is a "source of energy"?

6. Who is Arch Riker marrying?

7. When is Arch's wedding to take place?

8. Arch suggests to Qwill that he "and Polly take the plunge at the same time." What is Qwill's response to this?

9. What is the name of the retirement complex in Florida where Euphonia Gage lived?

10. What is the name of the WPKX meteorologist?

11. Junior Goodwinter was shocked by his grandmother's new passion for what?

12. What is the name of Euphonia Gage's next-door neighbor?

13. What is Nancy Fincher's maiden name, and who is her father?

14. Where did the state police find Gil Inchpot's truck?

15. Who owns Park of Pink Sunsets, and who manages it?

16. What is the name of the gentleman that had a crush on Mrs. Gage?

17. What does Euphonia Gage's will leave to Junior, Pug, and Jack?

18. To whom does Mrs. Gage leave everything? And for what purpose?

19. Qwill takes Koko "for a little ride along the shore . . . [to] see if the cabin's buttoned up for the winter." While driving, Koko "created a disturbance in the backseat . . . [and] in a frenzy . . . dashed about the interior of the car." What does Qwill do, and what does he discover?

20. Where does Qwill recall seeing Betty and Claude previously?

21. It was the "worst storm in the history of Moose County. . . . Three low pressure fronts . . . met and clashed over [the] . . . area." Just how many inches of snow were there?

22. What appears to be the "only valuable item" Koko finds in the Gage house closets?

23. Who is forced to play Santa Claus in the Christmas parade?

24. Qwill organizes "Operation Greenback" with Celia Robinson. There are four phases to this plan. Put them in the correct order.

_____ Celia's late sister was a collector of antiques. She is to ask the park management if they know how she can sell her sister's antiques with as little effort as possible. She also needs to sell her house.

_____ Celia has become the sole heir to her late sister's large house, valuable possessions, and considerable financial assets. She wants to share her good fortune with her neighbors by giving a

Christmas party in the clubhouse. She tells the management that she is willing to spend $5,000.

_____ Celia is to ask the management if she could move into a double-wide. She also seeks permission to keep her late sister's cat, who has a trust fund of $10,000.

_____ Celia buys a large plant for the park management office. She also tells them she will have a surplus of cash and asks if they know where she might invest the money.

25. When Koko drops a packet of foot powder at Qwill's feet, what does this cause Qwill to realize about many of the items Koko has been collecting from the closets?

26. What happened to Lena?

27. When Qwill asks Nancy Fincher if she remembers the date of the Christmas parade, she says she does. When was it, and why is Nancy sure of the date?

28. What does the date of Nancy's mother's birthday suggest to Qwill?

29. How did thieves know that Qwilleran would not be home the night they came to steal light fixtures and murals?

30. How does Qwill learn that Euphonia was being blackmailed? And why was she being blackmailed?

31. If Gil Inchpot were blackmailing Mrs. Gage, Qwill suggests that he had help. Who does Qwill believe was helping Inchpot?

Chronological Order of Events

Arrange the following events in their order of occurrence.

_____ Qwill moves into the Gage mansion.

_____ Koko looks at pictures of Mrs. Gage and her friends in Florida sent to Qwill by Celia Robinson. Koko "flicked his tongue at a couple of them."

_____ Koko and Yum Yum enjoy the many closets in the Gage mansion immediately.

_____ Euphonia Gage is found dead in bed at her Florida retirement village.

_____ Koko loses interest in the book *Robinson Crusoe*, he ignores the closets, and he never sits in the safe again.

_____ Qwill realizes that many of Koko's "finds" are related to feet.

_____ Qwill is snowed in at the Lanspeaks' and receives a call from Polly's sister-in-law that the cats are missing.

_____ Qwill presents in preview his docudrama of *The Big Burning of 1869*.

_____ Euphonia's will leaves a small amount for each grandchild and the rest to the Park of Pink Sunsets.

_____ Gage's attorney tries to contest her will but has no financial documents to support his case.

_____ Qwill puts it all together: Euphonia had a baby named Lethe; she paid a farm family to raise her; her name was changed to Lena; she was Nancy's mother; Nancy is Junior Goodwinter's cousin.

_____ Nancy Fincher takes Qwill across the Flats on her dogsled.

_____ Nick Bamba picks Qwill up and takes him to the mansion.

_____ Qwill discovers that someone is trapped in the elevator.

_____ Qwill confirms that all the "suicides" at Park of Pink Sunsets have been murders.

_____ Betty and Claude are found in Texas near the Mexican border, and Pete is arrested in Kentucky.

_____ Koko sniffs the bindings of books in the library and finally settles on *Robinson Crusoe*.

Koko and Yum Yum

1. Which cat is described as having a "degree of intelligence and perception" that is "unnerving to a human with only five senses and a journalism degree"?

2. When Qwill reads to the cats, who likes to choose the books?

3. Who does Mrs. Fulgrove accidentally lock in a closet?

4. What is the name of the Wilmots' cat, "a threat to Koko's territory . . . and interested in Yum Yum"?

5. What is the name of the black and white cat that Celia Robinson receives from Chicago?

Women in Qwill's Life

1. Where does Polly live now?

2. Who is "jealous of women younger and thinner than she"?

3. Arch Riker promotes Hixie Rice to a new position. What is it?

4. Why did Hixie study French briefly?

5. What does Qwill give Polly for Christmas?

Qwill's Living Quarters

1. Which feature made the Gage mansion unique?

2. Who was Qwill's landlord?

3. How many closets did Qwill count in the Gage mansion?

4. Match the room or feature of the Gage mansion to its description:
   a. foyer   b. woodwork   c. basement ballroom   d. main floor

   _____ "Coffered paneling of the high ceiling and the lavishly carved fireplaces"

   _____ Looks like "a luxury liner of early vintage"

   _____ The best on Goodwinter Boulevard

   _____ A "large, turn-of-the-century hall with Art Deco murals and light fixtures"

Dining Out

1. Match the food to the place where it is most likely served:

   a. Lois's Luncheonette   **c.** Tipsy's
   b. Buffet Table at the premier of   **d.** Thanksgiving Dinner
   The Big Burning of 1869

   _____ Broiled whitefish and steak that is an "old-fashioned cut of meat that required chewing"

   _____ Mince pie

   _____ Squash puree with cashews

   _____ Doughnuts which are "old-fashioned fried cakes with a touch of nutmeg"

   _____ "Hot turkey sandwich with mashed potatoes and gravy"

   _____ Buckwheat pancakes

   _____ "Fish House punch"

   _____ "Stuffed mushrooms, bacon-wrapped olives, cheese puffs"

   _____ Chinese tea with lemongrass

2. When Qwill picked the lock of the library closet, he found one of Lena's recipes. Which one was it?

Crimes and Victims

1. Does Qwill believe that Mrs. Gage was the first suicide at Park of Pink Sunsets?

2. What does Qwill suggest to Andy that the motto might be at Park of Pink Sunsets?

3. How does Qwill believe Euphonia Gage might have been killed?

4. Who does Qwill suggest killed Euphonia Gage?

5. Who does Qwill believe killed Gil Inchpot?

6. How was Gil Inchpot killed?

CHARACTER IDENTIFICATION III

Who is who? Can you identify the following characters?

1. The owner of a horse farm and the horse Son of Cardinal.

2. Old clairvoyant from Lockmaster who is a friend of Mildred Hanstable.

3. Principal of Pickax High School and director of *Henry VIII*. He is "eminently successful at everything."

4. Sisters who have 1,862 teddy bears.

5. Manager at the Casablanca. Qwill refers to her as "Madame Defarge."

6. Friend and next-door neighbor of Euphonia Gage at the Park of Pink Sunsets.

7. Celia Robinson's thirteen-year-old grandson.

8. Junior Goodwinter's brother and sister.

9. Junior Goodwinter's cousin in Moose County who breeds Siberian huskies. She has "wavy hair [and] . . . large brown eyes." She is "shy, [and] inarticulate. . . ."

10. A used-car salesman in Pickax who drop-ships a yellow sports car to Euphonia Gage in Florida.

11. She marries Arch Riker on Christmas Eve.

12. He's from Des Moines and was a partner with Dianne Bessinger for eighteen years in an art gallery. He was also her husband for several years.

13. He is the official historian for the county. He knows everyone in two counties.

14. VanBrook's former housekeeper, this lady played Queen Katharine in *Henry VIII*. She has a son, Robin.

15. This seventy-five-year-old's father built the Casablanca. She lives on the twelfth floor and never leaves her apartment. She loves table games.

16. He represented Forest Beechum at his murder trial.

17. He is the new chef at the New Pickax Hotel. Originally from Fall River, Massachusetts, he has a shaggy beard and wears a hair net when cooking.

18. Young jogger who is a bartender at the Penniman Plaza.

19. Designs and engineers the renovation of Qwill's apple barn.

20. Once married to Hugh Lumpton, she is the daughter of J.J.

21. Driver of the bus on the Bonnie Scots Tour.

22. This man and his wife run a "service network" for people on the list. You sign up, pay a fee, leave a key, and they send out a repairman.

23. She is a columnist for the *Spudsboro Gazette*. Her column is called "Potato Peelings," and her nickname is "Cookie."

24. He owns a men's store, talks with a brogue if he needs to, and tells Qwill that he "canna remember any dead bodies before you [Qwill] moved to town."

25. She's a volunteer at the Pickax Hospital and the chief canary at the Senior Care Facility. She killed her boyfriend when she was eighteen and was sentenced to twenty years. She received probation and was ordered to do ten years of community service.

CLUES, CLUES, CLUES III

Can you identify the mystery based on the list of clues provided?

1. "Orchard Incident"
   Red jelly beans
   Boxes coded with red dots
   Counterfeit money
   Qwill's book, *The City of Brotherly Crime*
   Apple tree wall hanging
   Stablechat
   Frozen rabbit

   _____

2. Missing financial records
   Robinson Crusoe
   Partial denture
   Birth certificate
   Marriage license
   Group picture
   Purple satin bedroom slipper
   Foot powder

3. Massachusetts license plate
   Tarot cards
   Bonnie Scots Tour
   Vitamin C tablets
   Emery boards
   Deglossed photographs
   Shredded obituary

4. Queen Anne chair
   Bottle of sherry
   Titled painting of mountains
   Black iron key
   "Hot Potato Fund"
   Scrapbook with editorial clippings

5. Sunken living room
   Flexible bracelet
   Scrabble tiles
   Table games
   Parking space #27
   Dynamite

PLACES, PLACES, PLACES III

How many places do you remember from your reading? See how many you can identify.

1. Small restaurant in Potato Cove with four kitchen tables and "some metal folding chairs . . ."

2. Business in Pickax City that handles Melinda Goodwinter's tag sale.

3. County seat in the Potato Mountains.

4. Small town in Moose County that was once the center of the lumbering industry.

5. This is a "slum of shacks and decrepit travel trailers, rusty vehicles, and ramshackled chicken coops."

6. A ghost town where artists on Little Potato settled in order to sell their works.

7. This is a "narrow peninsula curving into the lake to form a natural harbor on the northern shore of Moose County." Polly and Irma Hasselrich go bird watching here.

8. Road in the Potato Mountains at the top of which is Tiptop.

9. Where is the craft store, Vance the Village Smith?

10. Which store in Lockmaster sells gaudy sweatshirts, posters, and T-shirts?

11. Retirement complex in Florida where Euphonia Gage and Celia Robinson lived.

12. Pender Wilmot's law office is in this building.

13. Popular apartment complex for singles in Pickax.

14. Condos XYZ Enterprises is building in Brrr.

15. This is a new hotel Down Below that looks like an amusement park.

QWILL QUIZ III

What new things have you learned about Qwill? Take the quiz and find out.

1. What is the Purple Plum?
2. What accident was the turning point in Qwill's life?
3. According to Qwill, which jelly beans are the only ones worth eating?
4. Books, Books, Books. Qwill talks a lot about writing one book or another. Unfortunately, he is frequently distracted and doesn't write the book. Can you match the proposed book to the mystery?

   a. *The Cat Who Lived High*
   b. *The Cat Who Knew a Cardinal*
   c. *The Cat Who Moved a Mountain*
   d. *The Cat Who Wasn't There*
   e. *The Cat Who Went Into the Closet*

   _____ A proposal to write and edit a book on a teddy bear collection

   _____ A biography about J. J. Hawkinfield

   _____ A book about the adventures of Koko and Yum Yum

_____ A book about the Moose County mystery man, Hilary Van-Brook

_____ A book about the Casablanca

5. Why does Qwill go to the mountains?

6. Why does Qwill agree to play Santa Claus in the Pickax Christmas parade?

7. Where did Qwill sell ties? Baseball programs?

8. Does Qwill have any living relatives?

9. Qwill's interest in renovation was acquired while he lived in Junktown. True or False?

10. Qwill likes golfing and fishing. True or False?

11. While Qwill is on his trip to Scotland, what does he promise Riker that his first column from there will be about?

12. Qwill's activities appear to pivot around feeding the cats, "the one constant in his unstructured life." True or False?

THE FACTS ABOUT POLLY DUNCAN

1. What is Polly's official position with the Pickax City Library?

2. How long has Polly lived in Pickax?

3. What is Polly's father's name?

4. What did Polly's dad name her?

5. How many sisters does Polly have?

6. What is one of Polly's favorite colors?

7. What are the names of Polly's cats?

8. What does Polly recite while doing boring tasks around the house?

9. Polly possesses a handgun. True or False?

10. Why did Polly cut her visit to England short?

11. What is Polly's favorite pick-me-up?

12. What is Polly's college roommate's name?

THE FACTS ABOUT
THE RIKERS

1. When did Arch and Mildred get married?

2. What is Arch's position with the *Daily Fluxion*?

3. What was Arch's first wife's name?

4. To whom was Arch engaged before he married Mildred?

5. What is Arch's role with the *Moose County Something*?

6. If Arch could be any artist, whom does he want to be?

7. What subjects did Mildred teach? Where did she teach?

8. How many years did Mildred teach school?

9. What does Mildred do to make other people feel lucky?

10. What is the name of Arch and Mildred's beach house?

11. What is Arch learning how to do?

12. What collection did Arch lose in his divorce settlement with Rosie?

THE FACTS ABOUT FRAN (FRANCESCA) BRODIE

1. Where does Fran work?

2. Who is Fran's father?

3. What role did she play in *Henry VIII*?

4. What color is Fran's hair?

5. What is Fran's greatest passion?

6. What role did she play in *Hedda Gabler*?

7. From where does she receive a good job offer?

8. Fran directs the Pickax Theatre Club's *Arsenic and Old Lace* and *A Midsummer Night's Dream* productions. True or False?

9. Fran is half Qwill's age. True or False?

10. Fran is engaged to Dr. Prelligate. True or False?

THE CAT WHO CAME TO BREAKFAST

General Questions

1. What number was painted on the side of Nick Bamba's cabin cruiser?

2. Marketing surveys suggested that the name Pear Island was more appealing than Breakfast Island. True or False?

3. Where is Polly going to spend the final two weeks of her vacation?

4. What two incidents at the hotel prompt Qwill to reconsider his reluctance to spend some time on Pear Island?

5. What incident happened at the Bambas' B and B? What does Nick ask Qwill to do?

6. What two books did Qwill pack to take with him to the island?

7. What is the fourth incident that occurs on the island?

8. What is the name of the Bambas' B and B?

9. Which cottage did Qwill and the cats stay in?

10. What is the name of the bar in the Pear Island Hotel?

11. How many dining areas are there in the Pear Island Hotel? Name them.

12. Who is the director of community services for XYZ Enterprises?

13. What does Qwill buy at Antiques by Noisette?

14. What caused Qwill to suspect Noisette?

15. Who was in Four Pips prior to Qwill and the cats?

16. What discovery of Yum Yum's caused Qwill to reconsider what happened to the front steps of the Domino Inn?

17. Mr. Harding, when describing the past on Pear Island, refers to things as "B.C." What does "B.C." stand for?

18. Which family owns the Pines?

19. According to Harriet Beadle, what is the original name of Breakfast Island?

20. Where on the island do the islanders live?

21. Which island is which? To the mainlanders the island is referred to as _____ _____; on a map it is _____ _____; the natives call it _____ _____; and the millionaires called it _____ _____ _____.

22. Which number does Koko draw twice the first time he and Qwill play dominoes?

23. Who is going undercover for Qwill on the island?

24. What does Koko do in order to convince Qwill not to go visit the Island Experience?

25. When Qwill realizes he has lost his mosquito spray on the trail, he returns to find it. What else does he find there?

26. Where does Exbridge want to hold the Midsummer's Eve dance?

27. What is the fifth incident to happen on the island?

28. What does Derek's first message to Qwill say?

29. Yum Yum, with the assistance of Qwill, finds a "half-crumpled piece of paper" under the seat of the sofa. What is written on this paper? With whom does Qwill associate the paper? How?

30. When Koko draws dominoes with Qwill and Elizabeth looking on, matched to letters of the alphabet, what do they spell?

31. What does Elizabeth say about the gilded leather masks as she leaves Qwill's apartment?

32. What was Qwill's private name for his teacher, Miss Heath?

33. In a later discussion with Derek about the message he left for Qwill, what does Qwill learn about the people who ate gumbo?

34. Which nuts from the nut bowl does Koko scatter on the floor?

35. What is Qwill's theory about the disappearance of the three light-keepers?

36. What was the name of the hotel guest who drowned?

37. After "field" appears several times when Qwill and Koko play dominoes, what does Qwill finally discover the word is? What other words does he then recall fit with this new word?

38. What is June Halliburton's maiden name? Where is she from originally? What does her father do?

39. Who were wives number four and number five for Jack?

40. Qwill's records of the domino games provide us with many clues. Can you list the words that were helpful to Qwill as he attempted to solve the crimes?

Chronological Order of Events
Arrange the following events in their order of occurrence.

_____ Food poisoning causes hotel guests to become ill.

_____ Koko shreds the June calendar.

_____ A man drowns in the new hotel's pool.

_____ Qwill and the cats board #66 and head to Breakfast Island.

_____ Qwill checks into Domino Inn, Four Pips.

_____ A cabin cruiser blows up at the Pear Island marina and kills the owner.

_____ A step at Domino Inn collapses and a guest falls and breaks a rib.

_____ Nick Bamba convinces Qwill to visit the island and "snoop around."

_____ A Pear Island vacationer is shot while hang gliding.

_____ Qwill enlists the help of Derek Cuttlebrink for undercover work.

_____ Yum Yum finds a cumpled piece of paper on which the telephone number to "The Pines Gatehouse" appears.

_____ Elizabeth overhears Elijah accuse Jack of starting the fire that kills June Halliburton.

_____ Brodie tells Qwill that the man who drowned was George duLac from Florida.

_____ Koko takes all of the hazelnuts from the nut bowl and scatters them on the floor.

_____ June Halliburton dies when her cottage is set on fire.

🐾 Koko and Yum Yum

1. Which cat prefers to walk away while being brushed?

2. According to numerology, which cat is "aristocratic, scientific, and mentally keen"? Which one is "patient and independent, with strong will-power"?

3. Which cat discovers a rusty nail in a crevice?

🐾 Women in Qwill's Life

1. Who invites Polly to Oregon? What is this person's name and profession?

2. How many postcards does Qwill receive from Polly?

3. What is June Halliburton's position with the Moose County Schools?

4. What is June's job on Pear Island?

5. What is the important decision that Polly made while in Oregon?

🐾 Qwill's Living Quarters

1. How many rooms are there in the Bambas' B and B? Suites? Cottages?

2. Describe a door on one of the cottages.

3. Qwill's cottage at Domino Inn has a sitting room, bedroom, minikitchen, and screened porch. True or False?

4. Domino Inn was formerly a private lodge in the twenties. True or False?

🐾 Dining Out

Match the food to the place where it is served.

a. Corsair Room of the Pear Island Hotel   b. Domino Inn
c. Harriet Beadle's Café

_____ "Jambalaya, a savory blend of shrimp, ham, and sausage"

_____ Pecan pancakes with maple syrup and turkey-apple sausages

_____ Smoked salmon with scrambled eggs

_____ Brioches filled with chipped beef

_____ Sweet potato pecan pie

_____ Gumbo, "an incredibly delicious mélange of shrimp, turkey, rice, okra and the essence of young sassafras leaves"

_____ Vegetable soup and hot dogs with everything

🐾 Crimes and Victims

1. How many people died after eating the gumbo?

2. What was the name of the man who drowned in the hotel pool?

3. Who falls and breaks a rib when one of the steps at Domino Inn collapses?

4. Who does Qwill believe is committing the crimes on Breakfast Island? Why?

5. Who started the fire that killed June Halliburton?

6. Who is June Halliburton's father?

7. Why does Jack kill June?

8. Who helps Jack commit the crimes/accidents on the island?

THE CAT WHO
BLEW THE WHISTLE

🐾 **General Questions**

1. Who bought out Trevelyan Construction?

2. What did Trevelyan do with the money he made from the sale of his construction business?

3. Koko is busy pushing books off shelves again. Arrange the following books in the order Koko pushes them:

   _____ *Androcles and the Lion*
   _____ *The Idiot*
   _____ *The Panama Canal: An Engineering Treatise*
   _____ *Swiss Family Robinson*

4. Match the terms to their meanings:

   a. hog   **b.** hoghead   **c.** Rule G   **d.** whittling   **e.** wildcat

   _____ A runaway locomotive
   _____ Locomotive
   _____ Engineer
   _____ SC&L rule against drinking
   _____ Taking a curve at high speed and breaking the wheels

5. What does Qwill suggest he might write a book about?

6. Who does Polly hire to build her house?

7. Where does Floyd's secretary live?

8. Who did the renovation of the Party Train?

9. What is Floyd Trevelyan's secretary's name, and where is she from?

10. After talking to MacWhannell, does Qwill believe that Floyd had an accomplice?

11. When does Qwill begin to suspect that Floyd Trevelyan is dead?

12. Who is Eddie Trevelyan's helper? He wears a ponytail and is a stocky guy.

13. What is the name of Eddie's dog?

14. What does Qwill tell Eddie that he does for a living?

15. What type of part-time job does Qwill suggest to Celia Robinson?

16. What gift does Liz give Qwill?

17. What did Qwill and Celia decide to call their investigation?

18. What are Quack, Whistle, and Squawk?

19. What happened when Koko stepped into the pyramid?

20. What pretense does Qwill use to interview Ozzie Penn?

21. What does SC&L stand for?

22. When Qwill needed to collect his thoughts, he could walk around the apple barn. According to Derek Cuttlebrink, if Qwill walked twenty-eight laps around the rooms, he walked one mile. True or False?

23. What column that Qwill wrote was inspired by an oil painting "depicting a beach scene at the turn of the century"?

24. What information does Qwill ask Hixie to ask the manager of Indian Village about?

25. Who paid Fran when she redid Nella Hooper's apartment at Indian Village?

26. Who wrote the lyrics to the song "The Wreck of Old No. 9"?

27. Which clues lead Qwill to suspect that Floyd was buried under concrete?

28. Who does Qwill believe is Koko's favorite character in all of Shakespeare?

Chronological Order of Events
Arrange the events in their order of occurrence.

_____ The Theatre Club decides to do *A Midsummer Night's Dream*.

_____ Qwill interviews Fred Trevelyan.

_____ Qwill, Polly, and the Rikers ride the Lumbertown Party Train.

_____ The State Banking Commission padlocks the Lumbertown Credit Union.

_____ Koko stands on his hind legs and looks out toward the orchard when Polly's house is under construction.

_____ Eddie dies from injuries he received in the bulldozer accident.

_____ When Eddie Trevelyan visits Qwill, Koko reacts with a "hostile hiss."

_____ Derek, Fran, and Elizabeth set up a portable pyramid in Qwill's barn.

_____ Koko knocks *Androcles and the Lion* off the bookshelf.

_____ Koko jumps into Qwill's lap and digs furiously in the crook of his elbow.

_____ Koko rushes madly around the barn, throwing himself into the front door twice.

_____ Koko sits on the *Moose County Something*, which has an article about the scandal, and then "circled the newspaper in a stiff-legged dance—his death dance."

_____ In a game of Book! Book!, Koko selects *The Panama Canal*.

_____ Koko sits on a copy of a playscript Fran wants Qwill to read.

_____ Qwill opens the door of the barn, and Koko runs to the building site, where he begins to dig at the edge of the concrete slab.

_____ James Henry Ducker, a.k.a. Benno, is the victim of a stabbing at the Trackside Tavern.

_____ Qwill finally realizes that Nella is really Lionella. He calls Andy Brodie and tells him to start looking for a man named Lionel, who impersonated Nella.

Koko and Yum Yum

1. Which cat tries to steal the police chief's badge?

2. When Koko sits inside the portable pyramid, what happens?

3. While collecting his thoughts, Qwill walks around the barn-house in circles. What do the cats do when they see him doing this?

4. When the cats are eating, what portion of the meal does Koko usually leave for Yum Yum?

5. According to Qwill, which cat is the investigator, and which one is the kleptomaniac?

Women in Qwill's Life

1. Who calls Qwill "Chief" and provides the popular treat "Kabibbles," which the cats love?

2. Who is described as an "independent person" who is "efficient and briskly decisive," but when problems requiring solutions arise, she melts into "a puddle of bewilderment"?

3. Qwill is concerned that Polly is "_____ too much and _____ too little."

4. What happens to Polly?

5. Who is Polly's doctor?

6. After Polly's surgery, where does she decide to convalesce?

Qwill's Living Quarters

1. The apple barn has a fieldstone foundation. True or False?

2. The cats consider the spiraling ramps in the apple barn as an indoor track. True or False?

3. In the apple barn there is a spotlight that highlights a "huge tapestry hanging from a balcony railing." True or False?

4. In the apple barn there are windowsills that enable the cats to stand on their hind feet and look out through the glass. True or False?

Dining Out

1. Mildred Riker calls them "croutons toasted with Parmesan cheese, garlic salt, red pepper, and Worcestershire sauce." What are they?

2. Qwill and Ozzie Penn go to the Jump-Off for lunch. How did the Jump-Off get started?

3. Match the food items to the event.

   a. Qwill and Polly dine at the Palomino Paddock
   b. Dinner on the Lumbertown Party Train

   _____ She-crab soup
   _____ Sea scallops in saffron cream sauce
   _____ Chateaubriand
   _____ Jellied beef consommé
   _____ Cheesecake
   _____ Grouper
   _____ Stuffed mushrooms
   _____ Caesar salad

Crimes and Victims

1. What happened to James Henry Ducker?

2. Qwill suspects that Ducker's death is drug related. True or False?

3. Who is Ducker also known as?

4. To what is Eddie's loss of control of the bulldozer attributed?

5. How does Qwill believe Floyd Trevelyan was killed?

6. Who murdered Floyd Trevelyan?

7. Who was the accomplice in Floyd's murder?

8. Who shot Zap, the dog?

9. Who killed Benno and why?

10. Who masterminded the plot?

THE CAT WHO SAID CHEESE

🐾 General Questions

1. There is a mysterious woman registered at the hotel in Pickax City. What color is she always wearing?

2. What are the three memorable events depicted on the tear sheets hanging on the walls of the *Moose County Something* conference room?

3. Who owns the New Pickax Hotel?

4. For whom does Qwill buy the 1899 cookbook, *Delicious Dishes for Dainty Entertaining*, compiled by the Pickax Ladies' Cultural Society?

5. Qwill also buys himself a copy of *Great Cheeses of the Western World—A Compendium*. What does Qwill have to do with this book? Why?

6. How does Qwill manage to get Gustav Limburger to agree to sit down for an interview?

7. Polly is recuperating at her sister-in-law's house on Pleasant Street. What has this street been nicknamed?

8. Who visited Polly and brought her some mushroom soup?

9. In which program at the community college is Derek Cuttlebrink enrolled?

10. Koko dislodges Euell Gibbons's *Stalking the Wild Asparagus* while playing Book! Book! with Qwill. What was the chapter Qwill chose to read about?

11. What is the name of Gustav Limburger's hired helper?

12. Who manages the turkey farm underwritten by the K fund?

13. What is the name of the restaurant Lori Bamba plans to open on Stables Row?

14. Where does Qwill meet the mystery lady?

15. What is she reading? What does she tell Qwill to call her?

16. How did the mysterious woman happen to know about Moose County?

17. Which room of the hotel is bombed?

18. Who is killed in the explosion at the hotel?

19. Who does Qwill suspect was registered in Room 203 at the hotel?

20. What name did the mystery lady use on the hotel register?

21. Who are the two witnesses that can describe the bomb suspect?

22. Why is Aubrey Scotten's hair white?

23. According to Junior, who is Qwill's number-one fan in the newspaper office?

24. Pasty Facts. Check all that are correct.

      _____ Real pasty dough consists of lard and suet.
      _____ Authentic filling is cubed beef or pork.
      _____ Some cooks omit the rutabagas.

25. When Qwill counts the cats' whiskers, how many does each have?

26. Which new business on Stables Row engendered a militant right-wing protest? Why?

27. Which witness is gunned down?

28. How does Koko convey to Qwill that Lenny Inchpot might be in danger?

29. What are the two categories of pasties judged in the contest? Why did Mildred disqualify one of the pasties in the final round?

30. What is the final bid amount for Qwill's package in the celebrity auction? Who wins the package?

31. How did Aubrey's friend, the fisherman, die?

32. What is the fisherman's name?

33. Whom does Qwill interview for his column on mushrooms?

34. What does Qwill suspect might be in Fetter's collection of cookbooks?

35. Whom does Qwill enlist to help him find out whether the missing recipe notebook is in the Fetter collection?

36. Why does Qwill inquire about the person who cooked the pasty that Mildred disqualified from the final round? Who cooked it?

37. How much is the reward for information leading to recovery of Iris Cobb's recipe notebook?

38. Who gave Celia Iris Cobb's notebook?

39. What is the relationship of the dead fisherman, Vic Greer, to Aubrey Scotten?

40. Where did Aubrey hide the gun used to shoot Franklin Pickett?

41. Whom did Vic want Aubrey to shoot?

42. What was Ona Dolman's real name, and who was she?

43. When Gustav Limburger dies, to whom does he leave his estate, including the New Pickax Hotel?

🐾 Chronological Order of Events

Arrange the following incidents in their order of occurrence.

_____ Qwill visits with Elaine Fetter about mushrooms. She tells him she is writing a cookbook, and he suspects that in her collection is Iris Cobb's missing notebook of recipes.

_____ During the cheese tasting party, Koko reacts with a "Yow" when Brie is mentioned.

_____ Franklin Pickett, a downtown merchant, is shot.

_____ The New Pickax Hotel suffers damage from an explosion in Room 203.

_____ Lenny Inchpot and others sustain injuries from the explosion. His girlfriend is killed in the explosion.

_____ Koko and Qwill play Book! Book! and Koko selects *Stalking the Wild Asparagus.*

_____ Koko sits in front of the refrigerator where Qwill has placed a frozen turkey. When Qwill opens the door, Koko jumps into the refrigerator with the turkey.

_____ Koko stalks Yum Yum.

_____ Qwill receives a letter from Onoosh, who tells him that the man stalking her is the man that planted the bomb.

_____ A fisherman is found dead at one of the Scotten cabins on Black Creek.

_____ Qwill decides to prepare the frozen turkey but discovers something hidden inside.

_____ Celia Robinson finds Iris Cobb's notebook of recipes.

_____ Aubrey calls Qwill and tells him he is going to kill himself. Qwill invites him to the barn.

_____ Qwill discovers the final clue in the mystery when, while reading *The Frogs*, Koko yowls when Qwill gets to a reference of "sleeping in a wool blanket." He realizes that this was what upset the bees and caused them to sting Vic Greer.

_____ David Fetter returns the notebook of recipes.

_____ Qwill places an ad in the *Moose County Something* offering a reward of $10,000 for the return of Iris Cobb's notebook of recipes.

_____ Brodie reaches in the turkey and finds a small handgun.

_____ Onoosh Dolmathakia tells Qwill she is going to return to Pickax and open a Mediterranean restaurant.

_____ Qwill takes Polly to Boulder House in Trawnto for a celebratory dinner.

_____ Koko wins in a game of blink against Qwill, suggesting that Aubrey was innocent.

Koko and Yum Yum

1. Which cat's head is stuck in Mrs. Cobb's old cheese basket?

2. Bushy comes to take pictures of the cats for a calendar competition. Is he successful? Yes or No?

3. When there's a message on the answering machine, how does Koko demonstrate the urgency of the call?

4. Which two books played a key role in Koko's conveying clues to Qwill in this story?

5. What three cheeses cause Koko to "Yow" each time he hears them?

Women in Qwill's Life

1. What two reasons does Qwill give when people ask, "Why don't you and Polly—?"

2. Polly informs Qwill that the mystery lady came into the library and checked out some books on a temporary card. When Qwill asks Polly what kind of books she checked out, what is Polly's response?

3. What do the young clerks at the library call Polly?

4. Where does Polly plan to live when she leaves the Duncan homestead?

5. What does Polly plan to ask the K fund to provide the library?

Qwill's Living Quarters

1. What architectural structure sits on top of the apple barn?

2. What area in the apple barn is not open to the cats?

Dining Out

1. If you wanted to sample a variety of soups and you were on Stables Row, where would you go?

2. Unscramble the menu enjoyed by Qwill and Polly at the Boulder House Inn.

Gniusma ttour   Piutnr ffeousl
Sresuoi stkae   Ssamee dsee aadls
Hspnica ni llyoph tsypar   Pchdoae prsae
Ssrubsle stupsor htwi caaawry

3. What did Elaine Fetter bring to Polly when she stopped by to visit with her?

4. Which restaurant offers specials like roast rack of lamb with green peppercorn sauce, "shrimp in a saffron cream with sun-dried tomatoes and basil, served on fettucine," and crème brûlée?

Crimes and Victims

1. Who takes the bomb into the hotel?

2. Who is Vic Greer's ex-wife?

3. Who shot Franklin Pickett?

4. Who was supposed to kill Lenny Inchpot?

5. What happened to Greer?

6. How does Qwill resolve the fact that Aubrey did not purposely cause Greer's death?

THE CAT WHO
TAILED A THIEF

🐾 General Questions

1. Who does Chief Brodie suspect might be committing petty larceny?

2. What's the first book Koko knocks down?

3. What does Qwill trade his compact sedan for?

4. What does Carter Lee James call the style of the houses on Pleasant Street?

5. How much money is stolen from the Indian Village clubhouse?

6. Which shoe does Arch Riker put on first?

7. What did Polly give Qwill for Christmas?

8. What did Bootsie give Qwill for Christmas?

9. Who gave Qwill a copy of *The Old Wives' Tale* by Arnold Bennett?

10. Whose household furnishing "represented the taste of passing generations and the fads of recent decades: a little William Morris, a little Art Deco, a little Swedish modern, a little French provincial, a little Mediterranean"?

11. MacMurchie has five dirks. Which dirk does he plan to keep for himself?

12. Based on Clayton's description of the voice of the lady from the bank, who does Qwill suspect she really is?

13. Hixie Rice is collecting New Year's resolutions for the Indian Village newsletter. Who made the following resolutions?

    _____ To find a playmate for Bootsie.
    _____ To get married.
    _____ To write a book.
    _____ To lose thirty pounds.
    _____ To eliminate family newsletters.

14. Whose idea is it to have an Ice Festival?

15. What is the name of the new gourmet club in Pickax?

16. Where was Willard Carmichael when he was killed?

17. Why was Lenny Inchpot arrested?

18. What is the title of the book Qwill proposes to write in which he compiles Moose County legends, anecdotes, and scandals?

19. To whom does Fran suggest offering the lead role in the play *Hedda Gabler*?

20. Who owns a collection of dolls that Qwill has decided to use as a topic in a forthcoming column?

21. Where was the first doll ever to disappear from the Kemple collection found?

22. How much did Carter Lee James want up front from Gary Pratt in order to restore the hotel?

23. Where do Carter Lee James and Lynette plan to spend their honeymoon?

24. According to Lori Bamba, what does it mean when Koko "swish[es] his tail from side to side"?

25. Who is Red Cap?

26. In one of his columns, how many ways does Qwill suggest February can be pronounced?

27. What is Wetherby's real name?

28. What did one of the cats do to the wedding photos that appeared in the *Moose County Something*?

29. Who assists Qwill in securing Carter Lee James's portfolio?

30. How does Carter Lee end up with the stolen doll from the Kemple collection?

31. Who stole the silver-hilted dirk from MacMurchie?

32. What did Danielle give Lynette and Carter Lee for a wedding present?

33. Who does Qwill believe is the kleptomaniac? How does he arrive at this?

34. Who actually sent the check for $2,000 to cover the theft of the bridge club fund?

35. What did the K fund investigators discover regarding Carter Lee James?

36. Where does Qwill find all the ingredients he needs for margaritas?

37. While visiting with Carter Lee and Danielle at the barn, which properties does Qwill tell Carter Lee he has a personal interest in seeing restored?

38. After hearing the legend of Dank Hollow, followed by the tale constructed by Qwill, what did Carter Lee order Danielle to do?

39. What happens to Carter Lee as he attempts to grab the dirk and attack Qwill?

40. What happens to Carter Lee and Danielle when they attempt to get away?

Arrange the following events in their order of occurrence.

_____ Tracy admits giving Carter Lee one of the Kemple dolls, which was found in Lenny's Locker.

_____ There's an outbreak of petty larceny in Pickax.

_____ Lenny Inchpot is arrested based on an anonymous tip.

_____ Qwill suspects George A. Breze.

_____ Celia Robinson discovers that Breze is not the thief.

_____ Koko knocks the Russian novel *A Thief* off the bookshelf.

_____ The bridge club fund money is stolen from a cabinet in the Indian Village clubhouse.

_____ Qwill and Wetherby Goode chase Carter Lee and Danielle through the flooded country.

_____ Lynette Duncan, married to Carter Lee James, dies on her honeymoon in New Orleans.

_____ Qwill writes a tale about a scam that supposedly happened in Pickax.

_____ One of the cats spits up a hairball on Carter Lee and Lynette's wedding picture in the newspaper.

_____ Willard Carmichael is killed while in Detroit.

_____ While listening to the *Adriana Lecourvreur* opera, Qwill realizes that Carter Lee poisoned Lynette.

_____ Carter Lee orders Danielle to go to the car, and then he confronts Qwill.

_____ Amanda tells Qwill that she knows that Carter Lee didn't do some of the houses he says he did.

_____ The K fund can find no evidence that Carter Lee is actually involved with restoration or preservation of houses.

_____ Carter Lee is captured and arrested for murder and fraud.

_____ Danielle turns state's witness.

_____ Qwill finally understands why Koko has been hitting/slapping Yum Yum; Carter Lee hired a hit man to kill Willard!

🐾 Koko and Yum Yum

1. Which cat approaches food from the left?

2. Which cat positions his/her rear to the north when eating?

3. What is the name of the fly that Qwill and the cats chase around the living room?

4. Which cat has toys in a drawer that bounce, rattle, roll, and glitter?

5. Which cat's secret dream is to catch mice?

6. Which cat "specializes in thought transference"?

🐾 Women in Qwill's Life

1. What does Qwill give Polly for Christmas?

2. What does Polly give Qwill for Christmas?

3. What does Polly rename her cat after Qwill criticizes the name Bootsie?

4. What is Polly's new cat's name?

🐾 Qwill's Living Quarters

1. Why are Qwill and the cats not living in the barn this winter?

2. Where does Qwill decide to live during the winter?

3. In which condo does Qwill live?

4. Who furnishes the condo for Qwill?

5. Fran has the pine furniture stripped to what new color?

6. Which room does Qwill use as an office?

🐾 Dining Out

1. The menu for the Nouvelle Dining Club's first meeting. Complete each menu item by matching it with its accompaniment.

   _____ Smoked whitefish
   _____ Black bean soup
   _____ Roast tenderloin of lamb
   _____ Puree of Hubbard squash
   _____ Spinach and redleaf lettuce tossed
   _____ Baked apples

   a. with conchiglie (pasta shells)
   b. in a crust of pine nuts, mushrooms, and cardamom
   c. on triangles of spoon bread with mustard broccoli coulis
   d. and leeks
   e. with ginger vinaigrette and garnished with goat cheese
   f. with peppercorn sauce

2. How many ways is Polly trying to "glamorize a flattened chicken breast"?

3. Where do Qwill and Willard Carmichael enjoy hummus, lentil soup, *tabbouleh* as the salad course, and shish kebabs, stuffed grape leaves, and spicy walnut cake?

4. Tonight there is one waiter and one choice on the menu: fried fish sandwich with lumbercamp fries and coleslaw. Where are we eating?

🐾 Crimes and Victims

1. Who was the first victim? What happened to this victim?

2. Who killed Carmichael?

3. What did Koko do repeatedly that finally caused Qwill to suspect that Carter Lee had hired a hit man to kill Carmichael?

4. What causes Lynette's death?

5. When Carter Lee is arrested, what is he charged with?

6. What happens to Danielle?

7. Which three books did Koko use to suggest clues to Qwill?

THE CAT WHO
SANG FOR
THE BIRDS

🐾 General Questions

1. When Qwill stops in Edd's Editions, what book does he buy?

2. To draw attention to the vandalism to the Coggin farmhouse, what book did Koko shove from the bookshelves?

3. How old do you have to be in Moose County to receive a free subscription to the *Moose County Something*?

4. What happened to the house Polly was building before she became ill?

5. What is the name of the Art Center manager?

6. What is the name of the butterfly girl's parrot?

7. Who is Paul Skumble?

8. Whose idea is it to have an adult spelling bee?

9. While browsing in Eddington's, Qwill buys three books from an estate on Purple Point. What are the titles?

10. What is the butterfly girl's boyfriend's name?

11. What is the butterfly girl's real name?

12. If Qwill could be any artist, whom did he want to be?

13. Who won the intaglio by W. C. Wyckoff?

14. When Koko jumped at the door handle on the broom closet, what was he trying to tell Qwill?

15. When Koko and Qwill discover the door to the Art Center is open, what do they find on the floor between the manager's office and the butterfly girl's studio?

16. What was missing from the open bin?

17. Frobnitz was one of the raffle winners in the Art Center contest. Who was the other winner?

18. Koko senses new books from Eddington's, and when he smells them, which book does he dislodge from the bookshelves?

19. Coincidentally, what happens later the same night that Koko dislodged the book *Fire Over London*?

20. Which of Calvert's photos did Koko lick?

21. When Rollo McBee finds the buried can, what is inside?

22. Who purchased Maude Coggin's land? What was the agreement made with her?

23. Qwill decides to write a column on "the ample moustache." Coincidentally, on which book is Koko sitting while Qwill is writing this column?

24. What was the subject of Duffield Campbell's watercolors?

25. Mr. Ramsbottom has apparently promised the manager's position to two people at the same time. Who are they?

26. At bedtime, when Qwill was reading Rebecca West's *The Birds Fall Down*, what did Koko do?

27. What are California Dogface, Hungarian Jester, Queen Alexandra Birdwing, and Orange Albatross?

28. Which book gave Qwill his idea for the format of the spelling bee? What had Koko been doing prior to this?

29. Who is Monkey?

30. Who owns the Northern Land Improvement company?

31. When Phoebe arrived late at the warm-up for the spelling bee, what raised suspicion that there was something wrong with her?

32. How much did the city council offer to pay Northern Land Improvement Company per acre for the cemetery expansion?

33. What happens to Qwill's seventeenth-century compass when Koko approaches it?

34. Who is Martha V. Snyder?

35. Who is Roy Gumboldt? What is his relationship to Chester Ramsbottom?

36. When Qwill is honored for his support of every local endeavor, what does he receive as a gift?

37. How does Qwill know that the Coggin farmhouse was torched?

38. What gift does Qwill give the parting Art Center manager, Beverly Forfar?

39. What are the winning names for the two adopted cats at the library?

🐾 Chronological Order of Events
Arrange the following events in their order of occurrence.

_____ Koko jumps at the broom closet handle, his way of telling Qwill he wants to go out.

_____ Qwill buys a copy of the 1939 *The Day of the Locust* by Nathaniel West.

_____ Koko licks Calvert's picture of Mrs. Coggin digging in the barnyard.

_____ Phoebe writes a letter to Qwill telling him she is going to her grandmother's in California.

_____ Qwill takes Koko to the Art Center, where they encounter an intruder.

_____ Koko jumps on the back of the intruder, and Qwill hits him on the head with a totem pole.

_____ While Qwill is reading _The Birds Fall Down_ by Rebecca West, Koko jumps up and bites his thumb.

_____ Someone has painted the word _witch_ on Mrs. Coggin's farmhouse.

_____ One evening, Koko selects the book _Fire Over London_ for reading.

_____ Koko awakens Qwill by thumping on his bedroom door. Qwill discovers that the Coggin farmhouse is on fire.

_____ Qwill and Koko discover the door to the Art Center open and blood on the floor.

_____ Fire Chief Gumboldt believes Mrs. Coggin's fire was an accident. Others believe it was arson.

_____ Qwill and Rollo McBee believe Mrs. Coggin buried her money in a coffee can in the yard.

_____ Hasselrich, Bennett and Barter open the coffee can and discover one hundred thousand dollars.

_____ Rollo finds a buried coffee can.

_____ Phoebe Sloan is killed in an accident in the Bloody Creek Gorge.

_____ Qwill realizes that two of the books Koko keeps knocking off the shelf are written by authors named West.

_____ Phoebe returns the missing drawings to the Art Center, and Jake abuses her.

_____ When Qwill shows his seventeenth-century compass to Thornton Haggis, Koko causes the north star on the compass to point west.

_____ Phoebe overhears Jake ask Chet for more money.

_____ Chet reminds Jake that he lit the match that burned Mrs. Coggin's house.

_____ Westrup is captured.

_____ The K fund buys the Coggin property and puts it in agricultural conservation.

🐾 Koko and Yum Yum

1. How does Qwill get the cats to and from the gazebo?

2. Which cat likes to bat insects against the screens?

3. With which sound does Koko answer the woodpecker?

   _____ Aaaaaaaaaaaaaaa
   _____ Kek-kek-kek-kek

4. The cats like to chase each other up and down the ramp inside the barn. How long does it take them to chase each other up the ramp and then down?

5. After a noontime treat of Kabibbles, how many licks, swipes, and passes do the cats make over each paw?

🐾 Women in Qwill's Life

1. What gift does Paul Skumble give Polly?

2. What color dress does Polly decide to wear in the portrait?

3. What book is Polly going to hold in her hand in the portrait painted by Skumble?

4. Because Polly works during the day, when has Paul Skumble decided to paint Polly's portrait?

🐾 Qwill's Living Quarters

1. What does Thornton Haggis call Qwill's apple barn?

2. How many sides does Qwill's gazebo have?

3. Who develops an avian garden near the gazebo?

Dining Out

1. How did Qwill know that the eggs in the mushroom frittata were cholesterol-free?

2. At which restaurant does Qwill find his choices to be pork, beef, or turkey, sandwich or platter, and hot-mild, hot-hot, or call 911?

3. Place the following food items on the correct restaurant menu:

    a. Palomino Paddock   b. Onoosh's Café   c. Old Stone Mill

    _____ Lamb shank with baked chickpeas

    _____ Tenderloin of ostrich with smoked tomatoes

    _____ Chilled gazpacho

    _____ Quail stuffed with mushroom and prune duxelle

    _____ Vegetarian stuffed grape leaves

    _____ Roasted red snapper with étouffée sauce and spinach

    _____ Vegetarian curry

    _____ Herbed polenta and black currant coulis

Crimes and Victims

1. Which book is Koko's clue to Qwill that Mrs. Coggin's house will burn?

2. How was Phoebe Sloan killed?

3. What clues did Koko give Qwill to implicate Jake Westrup in the crimes?

4. Who killed Phoebe?

5. When Jake was arrested, what was he charged with?

6. When Koko and Qwill hear the intruder in the Art Center, what does Qwill strike the intruder with? What does Koko do to the intruder?

7. What was Koko's clue to Qwill that he should consider Ramsbottom as a suspect?

8. What will happen to Ramsbottom?

CHARACTER IDENTIFICATION IV

Who is who? Can you identify the following characters?

1. President of the Lumbertown Credit Union.

2. Polly's assistant at the Pickax Library.

3. Trawnto Beach resident who wins first place for a turnipless pasty.

4. Assigned to cover the Lumbertown Credit Union scandal and to interview Gustav Limburger.

5. A dowser who is retired from the plumbing and hardware business.

6. Also known as Big Mac.

7. He is planning to marry Celia Robinson.

8. Cheese expert of the Sip 'n' Nibble Shop.

9. Wine expert of the Sip 'n' Nibble Shop.

10. Contributed the story about the Dimsdale Jinx for Qwill's book *Short & Tall Tales*.

11. The so-called cousin of Danielle Carmichael.

12. An eye-catching beauty from Texas who is the secretary at the Lumbertown Credit Union.

13. Eddie Trevelyan's friend who wears a ponytail and is from Chipmunk. He is also known as Benno.

14. Retired schoolteachers who live at the retirement village at Ittibittiwassee Estates.

15. Office manager of the *Moose County Something*. She gives Qwill a leather-bound copy of *The Old Wives' Tale* by Arnold Bennett.

CLUES, CLUES, CLUES IV

Can you identify the mystery based on the list of clues provided?

1. *The Day of the Locust*
   The Crucible
   Fire Over London
   Coffee can
   Seventeenth-century compass
   Arson

   _____

2. *A Midsummer Night's Dream*
   Hermia
   Black felt-tip pen
   Duck decoys
   Androcles and the Lion
   Vigils at the windows

   _____

3. Calendar
   Food poisoning
   Explosion
   Hazelnuts
   Chicken gumbo
   Resort development

   _____

4. *Stalking the Wild Asparagus*
   Brie, gruyere, feta
   A Taste of Honey
   Handgun
   Turkey farm
   Wool blanket

   _____

5. Gastrointestinal complications
   Petty larceny
   The Thief
   Hoax
   The Confidence Man
   Kemple dolls

   _____

PLACES, PLACES, PLACES IV

How many places do you remember from your reading? See how many you can identify.

1. Business on Pear Island owned by Noisette duLac.

2. Chet Ramsbottom's business in Kennebeck.

3. A block-long stone building in Pickax remodeled to accommodate several shops.

4. Lori Bamba's new restaurant, which serves different soups.

5. "Strictly a male hangout," this bar is in Sawdust City.

6. Store in Pickax where Qwill buys an occasional tie and his kilt.

7. Wine and cheese shop in Stables Row.

8. Bank managed by J. Willard Carmichael.

9. This is the "central intelligence agency" of Pickax and "a daycare facility for grandparents."

10. A new resort that is developed by XYZ Enterprises and funded by the K fund.

11. The first ethnic restaurant in Pickax.

12. This expensive restaurant, a "mix of sophistication and hayseed informality," is located near Whinny Hills.

13. Lockmaster company that buys Mrs. Coggin's property.

14. The new gourmet club in Pickax that is "committed to quality rather than quantity."

15. New college located in the vacant houses on Goodwinter Boulevard.

16. Run-down mansion with exterior brickwork and stately windows with "stained-glass transoms . . . and beveled glass."

17. An event in Moose County that celebrated all kinds of foods. There was a cooking class for men, a street dance, a celebrity auction, and the official opening of Stables Row.

18. Space on the lower level of the Art Center used to display photography.

19. Official headquarters for the Ice Festival. This barrackslike building is in Mooseville.

QWILL QUIZ IV

What new things have you learned about Qwill? Take this quiz and find out.

1. What type of opera does Qwill tell Polly he is thinking about writing?

2. Where has Qwill seemingly found "middle-age contentment"?

3. What does Qwill call the owl in his orchard?

4. Qwill does "his best thinking with his _____ elevated, a legal pad in his _____ hand and a black felt-tip in his _____."

5. Qwill's motto is "_____ to bed and _____ to rise."

6. What does Qwill plan to call the book for which he is collecting "Moose County legends, anecdotes, and scandals"?

7. What would Qwill "have given anything to be"?

8. Whom does Qwill consider the pair of bookends "supporting the volumes of his life"?

9. Qwill buys a cell phone so that he can call the city desk at the *Moose County Something*. True or False?

10. Qwill uses a word processor to write his columns. True or False?

11. Check all the topics below on which Qwill has considered writing a book:

    _____ Steam Age of Railroading
    _____ Cheese
    _____ Dowsing
    _____ Moose County Legends
    _____ Pickax Hotel
    _____ Mushrooms
    _____ Eggs
    _____ Snowshoeing
    _____ Sunburn

12. Check all the topics below on which Qwill has written a column:

    _____ Aurora borealis
    _____ Corn
    _____ Sunbathing
    _____ Pencils
    _____ Santa Claus
    _____ Lynette
    _____ Naming cats
    _____ Nobodies
    _____ Dowsing
    _____ Old pasty recipes

THE FACTS ABOUT HIXIE RICE

1. In what language does Hixie like to drop phrases?

2. What is Hixie's position with the *Moose County Something*?

3. When Arch promotes Hixie, to what position does he promote her?

4. Hixie produces and directs *The Big Burning of 1869*. True or False?

5. Hixie has had some "brilliant" ideas. Can you arrange the ideas in their order of occurrence in the series?

    _____ Annual Mark Twain Festival
    _____ Shafthouse Motorcade and Dedication
    _____ Adult spelling bee
    _____ Moose County Ice Festival
    _____ Pickax Sesquicentennial

THE FACTS ABOUT DEREK CUTTLEBRINK

1. Just how tall is Derek? Three different heights have been given. Do you remember?

2. Where does he go to college? What is he studying there?

3. Check all the career options Derek has considered:

   ____ Teacher   ____ Cook/food service

   ____ Law enforcement   ____ Stockbroker

   ____ Actor   ____ Musician

   ____ Ecologist

4. How many minor roles did Derek play in *Henry VIII*?

5. What role did Derek play in *Visit to a Small Planet*?

6. Who writes the lyrics to Derek's songs?

7. What is Derek's position at Owen's Place in Mooseville?

8. Who is his current girlfriend (as of *The Cat Who Blew the Whistle*)?

9. For which team does Derek spell in the spelling bee sponsored by the Pickax Theatre Club?

10. What is his job in the Mackintosh Room at the Mackintosh Inn?

CATS, CATS, CATS

Whose is whose? To whom do these cats belong?

1. Brutus

2. Bootsie

3. Flora

4. Carrie and Charlotte

5. Katie and Mac

6. Jet Stream (a.k.a. Jet-boy)

7. Louisa May

8. Punkin

9. Nicodemus

10. Sarah

11. Toulouse

12. Winston

THE CAT WHO
SAW STARS

🐾 General Questions

1. Where did the missing backpacker store his gear prior to his disappearance?

2. Who wrote the feature "Missing Hiker Baffles F'Port?"

3. What was the missing backpacker's first name?

4. Qwill's readership was over 90 percent—more than that of the daily horoscope. True or False?

5. From whose point of view did Qwill write about the Fourth of July?

6. Which three Twain works did Eddington find for Qwill?

7. What was the name of the play selected by the Pickax Theatre Club to open their summer season?

8. Where is Polly vacationing? With whom is she vacationing?

9. What is the name of the private club where the Rikers' beach house is located?

10. What is the name of the Rikers' bungalow?

11. What is Arch learning to knit?

12. What is the name of Qwill's new guest accommodations?

13. What is the name of the thoroughfare that slices "through the Great Dunes"?

14. Signing of the Declaration of Independence, Dear Old Golden Schoolboys, Friends of Wool, and Feedin' the Chickens are examples of what?

15. Who discovers the buried body of the hiker?

16. What was the hiker's name, how old was he, and where was he from?

17. How long had the hiker been dead? What was unusual about the condition of the body?

18. What was the hiker's hobby?

19. What is the best-selling lunch item at Owen's Place?

20. On whom did Lisa Compton's great-grandmother have a crush?

21. What did Rebecca Hawley present to Qwill when he visited her at the Safe Harbor Residence?

22. When Elizabeth did a rune reading for Ernestine, why didn't she share the results with her?

23. What is Polly's sister's name? This name is short for what other name?

24. What is the name of Bushy's boat?

25. What is the name of Owen and Ernie Bowen's boat?

26. To what does Bushy attribute the loose sand that has "blown up into a ridge, all the way from Fishport to Purple Point"?

27. What was the connection between Koko's interest in Mark Twain's novella *A Horse's Tale* and the death of Owen Bowen?

28. Qwill agrees to support a project proposed by Dr. Teresa Bunker. What is the project?

29. What is Arch's nickname?

30. While hanging the four-foot wheel over the fireplace, what does Qwill discover on the surface of the mantel?

31. Can you name the four plays that Polly and her sister saw?

32. To which two postcards did Koko give his seal of approval?

33. For what position is Amanda Goodwinter preparing to run?

34. What is the name of Phil Scotten's dog?

35. What does Scotten's dog, a retired G-dog, do when he sniffs while aboard the *Suncatcher*?

36. What does Koko keep doing to one of the skewers?

37. What does Qwill instruct the florist to say in the card that accompanies the bouquet of flowers he is sending to Polly?

38. What type of books will be housed in Elizabeth's lending library?

39. To whom do the plays *Major Barbara* and *The Importance of Being Earnest* refer?

40. Which book that Qwill has been reading coincidentally predicted the sinkhole?

41. Who is Ms. Gamma?

42. Where was the alleged crime?

43. What did Polly bring Qwill from Canada?

Chronological Order of Events

Arrange the following events in their order of occurrence.

_____ Barb tells Qwill that Ernie discovered what Owen was doing, and he threatened her. She used a potato skewer to kill him.

_____ Barb admits to Qwill that she had been dating Owen.

_____ Koko tries to prevent Qwill from leaving the cabin in Mooseville.

_____ Ernie dies when her RV drops in the sinkhole and she is buried under the sand.

_____ Qwill discovers a crack along the mantel when he hangs the wagon wheel.

_____ Qwill and Bushy observe the *Suncatcher* tied up next to the *Fast Mama*.

_____ Koko leaves fang marks on two of the postcards Polly sent Qwill from Canada.

_____ Qwill's moustache twitches when he realizes why Koko has been interested in the postcards of Wilde and Shaw.

_____ A sinkhole opens up behind Owen's Place.

_____ Tess notices that one of the potato skewers has been knocked off the wall.

_____ Qwill meets Phil Scotten and his dog, Einstein. They inspect the *Suncatcher*. Einstein sits down like he is supposed to do when he discovers drugs.

_____ Owen Bowen drowns while on the lake with his wife, Ernie.

_____ Koko chooses the book *A Horse's Tale*.

_____ An unidentified backpacker is missing.

_____ Koko insists on going for a walk on the beach.

_____ Qwill and Koko discover the body of the backpacker buried in the sand.

_____ The Hawleys identify the body as that of the backpacker.

_____ The coroner can't identify the cause of the backpacker's death, and the body is sent to the state forensic lab.

Koko and Yum Yum

1. Which cat enjoys a brushing?

2. Which cat considers brushing a game of "fight-the-brush"?

3. Why don't the cats like to roll on the concrete floor of the lakeside porch?

4. Which cat frees the hummingbird whose beak is caught in the porch screen?

5. Who is Gertrude?

6. Of which cat does Bushy finally get a picture?

🐾 Women in Qwill's Life

1. Why does Polly send Qwill a postcard every day?

2. Who is the corvidologist that visits Qwill?

3. Initially Qwill is anxious for his houseguest to leave. What causes him to change his mind?

4. When Polly says she won't ask Qwill to explain the presence of the "aggregation of youthful pulchritude" present the day she returned from Canada, Qwill replies that he won't ask her to explain what?

5. When Mildred asks Qwill why he and Polly don't get married, Qwill replies that she drinks _____ and he drinks _____.

🐾 Qwill's Living Quarters

1. According to Qwill, the old cabin at Mooseville is more "psychological than geographic." True or False?

2. Qwill refers to the screened porch as "Cloud Nine." True or False?

3. How many skylights are there in the old cabin?

4. What is the sandladder that leads to the beach?

5. Why isn't the new guest house "too comfortable or too attractive"?

6. This building, the same size as the toolshed, has windows, indoor plumbing, and modular furniture. What is it?

🐾 Dining Out

Match the meal or menu item to the location.

a. Breakfast at the Rikers
b. Linguini's
c. Northern Lights Hotel

d. Owen's Place
e. Qwill's cabin
f. Dinner at the Rikers

_____ Butternut and roasted pepper soup, coddled pork chops, twice-baked potatoes, broccoli soufflé, Waldorf salad, pinot noir, and Black Forest cake

_____ "Lamb shank osso bucco on a bed of basil fettuccini"

_____ Skewered potato with your choice of one sauce

_____ "Grilled petite tenderloin of venison with smoked bacon, braised cabbage strudel, and a sun-dried Bing cherry demiglaze"

_____ Pecan waffles, apple-chicken sausages, and blueberry muffins

_____ Veal marsala, stuffed manicotti, and lasagna

_____ Thimbleberry pancakes, duck egg omelettes with mushrooms, and "lamb shank with beans, lumberjack style"

_____ Ham and cheese sandwich and a cup of cream of tomato soup

Crimes and Victims

1. Do we know exactly how David died?

2. What happens to Ernie Bowen?

3. What does the evidence suggest about Owen?

THE CAT WHO
ROBBED A BANK

🐾 General Questions

1. What two festivals are about to take place in Pickax and the surrounding counties?

2. What does Culvert McBee give Qwill?

3. There were four Goodwinter brothers who founded Pickax in 1850. True or False?

4. Gregory Blythe is the current mayor of Pickax. True or False?

5. What is the name of the play the Pickax Theatre Club is opening its season with?

6. Each day on Culvert's calendar features a saying. What do all of the sayings have in common?

7. What will the new name of the presidential suite at the hotel be?

8. What is the hotel's new name?

9. The interior is furnished in the Arts and Crafts period. What designer is the American leader of the Arts and Crafts movement?

10. Who painted the portrait of Anne Mackintosh Qwilleran hanging in the foyer of the Mackintosh Inn?

11. What is the name of the new manager of the inn?

12. What is the name of the lady who supposedly haunts Qwill's carriage house?

13. How many cats does Magdalene Sprenkle have?

14. Sprenkle's cats are named after famous women. Can you complete the name chart below?

Sarah _____
Charlotte _____
Carrie _____
Flora _____
Louisa May _____

15. Fishport is known as the "home of the _____ _____."

16. Qwill wants to attend Delacamp's tea. How does he propose going?

17. What does Qwill buy at the craft fair?

18. What are the initials on the bottom of the spalted maple bowl?

19. Who is traveling with Delacamp this time?

20. Who will be pouring tea for Delacamp?

21. What is the name of the perfume that Qwill wants to give to Polly as a surprise?

22. Qwill told Polly to select something for herself as a Christmas gift. What did Polly find?

23. What is the name of the hotel night clerk?

24. What is the name of Delacamp's supposed niece?

25. When does Qwill first suspect that Delacamp was smothered?

26. What did Maggie Sprenkle observe from her window on the night of Delacamp's murder?

27. What is strange about the disappearance of Delacamp's niece?

28. The Scottish Games: Which event is which?

    a. Tossing the caber   b. Throwing the box   c. Putting the stone
    d. Heaving the sheaf   e. Throwing the hammer

    _____ A burlap sack filled with twenty pounds of hay is lifted with a pitchfork and pitched over a crossbar.

    _____ The thrower stands with his back to the goal and his feet planted firmly on the ground. He twirls and lets it fly.

    _____ This feat is performed with a twenty-foot cedar log weighing more than a hundred pounds.

    _____ A fifty-six-pound box weight with a ring attached has to be thrown over a bar.

    _____ This event requires the contestant to balance a stone ball with one hand at shoulder height, then heave it.

29. What gift did Mildred give Qwill?

30. Who drops pennies here and there for someone else to find?

31. What does Carol Lanspeak's housekeeper discover is missing from the powder room?

32. Who is Polly's new neighbor?

33. What does Koko do with the pencils he takes out of the ceramic pencil holder?

34. Where does Qwill put pennies he finds?

35. What item was missing from both bathrooms in Delacamp's room?

36. Where does Boze tell Lenny he is going? How is he getting there?

37. Whose collection of mechanical banks was Susan Exbridge liquidating?

38. Which collectible mechanical bank is Qwill interested in?

39. When Osmond Hasselrich died, what did he want Qwill to have?

40. What does Boze steal from Deputy Greenleaf?

41. Who hijacked the Pickax Library's bookmobile?

42. What was Qwill's father's name?

43. Possible titles for The Absolutely Absurd Press, Inc., include: *Recipes for Entertaining by Lurcretia Borgia, My Secret Life as a Pussycat* by King Kong, and *Icabod Crane's Low-Fat Cookbook.* Who suggested each title?

44. What is Boze's real name? What is his mother's name?

45. What happened to Boze's father? Who was his father?

46. Which book that interests Koko does Qwill find coincidental to what he learns about Boze (Donald)?

47. What does Koko find under the rug in the foyer?

48. When Lenny and Qwill go looking for Boze, how does Lenny know that Boze has been there?

49. What happened to Qwill's father?

50. What was Delacamp's supposed niece's real name?

🐾 Chronological Order of Events
Arrange the events in their order of occurrence.

_____ Delacamp is coming to Pickax again.

_____ Late one night, Koko yowls outside Qwill's bedroom door.

_____ Koko tosses his own cabers: yellow pencils with fang marks in them.

_____ Nora tells Qwill a story about a girl named Betsy and her son Donald.

_____ Boze tells Lenny that he "took care of the old guy."

_____ Culvert gives Qwill a calendar.

_____ Qwill gets a preview of the newly refurbished and renamed hotel, now Mackintosh Inn.

_____ Koko unfurls two rolls of paper towels in Qwill's kitchen.

_____ Qwill and Lenny go to Big B Mine.

_____ Lenny knocks out the deputy and takes her gun. Then he hijacks the library bookmobile.

_____ Koko scatters Brazil nuts on the floor.

_____ Koko studies the pictures of the Scottish Gathering and licks three pictures of Boze.

_____ Qwill buys a mechanical bank for the Sprenkle collection.

_____ Boze commits suicide.

_____ Bart calls to tell Qwill that Delacamp died in his sleep.

_____ Qwill understands the significance of Koko's interest in _Oedipus Rex_.

_____ Koko pushes the play _Night Must Fall_ off the table in an attempt to get Qwill to read it.

_____ The police find Boze's body.

_____ Becky Ditcher, who works at the inn, finds Delacamp in his bed with a pillow over his head.

_____ Harriet Marie Penney is arrested as she tries to board a plane for Rio with jewelry and cash.

Koko and Yum Yum

1. Which cat is the "brains of the family"?

2. Which cat is the "glamorcat"?

3. Which cat can "shriek like an ambulance siren"?

4. Which cat can sense when the telephone is going to ring?

5. Why does Qwill buy a Chinese water bucket and use it as a trash can?

6. What do the cats do when their bedtime snack is late?

Women in Qwill's Life

1. What gift does Polly give Qwill on Father's Day?

2. Qwill and Polly wear Scottish attire to the charity benefit for literacy. What does Polly wear?

3. What purchase that Qwill made from Delacamp's firm allowed Polly to be "in the inner circle" and asked to pour tea at Delacamp's Tuesday Tea?

4. What perfume does Qwill special-order from Lanspeak's to mark the occasion when he and Polly spent an evening when "twilight descended on the world like a blue mist and brought a magical silence"?

Qwill's Living Quarters

1. What shape are the windows in the apple barn?

2. On which side of the apple barn are the front doors that open into the foyer?

Dining Out

1. Where do Qwill and Polly enjoy baba ghanouj and spanakopitas as appetizers?

2. Celia brings Qwill and the cats two of their favorite foods. What are they?

3. Which host prepares his/her "famous breast of duck with prosciutto and mushroom duxelles"?

4. What are bridies?

5. What is New Century Dining?

6. Who sends Qwill some tuna salad, ham loaf, and bread pudding "laced with chocolate sauce"?

7. Who serves "individual casseroles of shrimp and asparagus, green salad with toasted sesame seeds and Stilton cheese, and cranberry parfaits"? What is the occasion?

8. What is the name of the coffee shop/dining room in the Mackintosh Inn?

Crimes and Victims

1. Who murdered Delacamp?

2. Match the clues.

a. Boze   c. smothering Delacamp
b. towels   d. Harriet Marie Penney

_____ Koko unfurling two rolls of paper towels
_____ *Oedipus Rex*
_____ *Night Must Fall*
_____ Yellow pencils
_____ Pennies
_____ Snapshots of the Highland Games

3. What happened to Boze?

THE CAT WHO SMELLED A RAT

🐾 General Questions

1. What was the three-day blizzard called "400 miles north of everywhere"?

2. What gift did Kirt Nightingale give Polly as a thank-you for inviting him to a simple supper?

3. How did residents of Indian Village persuade Don Exbridge to fix the leaking roofs?

4. Whose idea was it to stage the Shafthouse Motorcade?

5. How many abandoned mines were there in Moose County? How far back did some date?

6. Qwill is interested in Egypt. What book did he buy from Eddington?

7. What do Maggie Sprenkle, Jess Povey, Amanda Goodwinter, Leslie Bates Harding, and Burgess Campbell have in common with each other?

8. When Arch suggests that Qwill write an advice column for the *Something*, what does he suggest he call it?

9. Who is the new batik artist in town? To whom is she related?

10. Who donated the bronze plaques identifying each of the mines?

11. At the auction, what does Qwill buy?

12. What did Qwill really want to buy at the auction?

13. What happens to Eddington Smith?

14. Who are the two new dermatologists in Pickax?

15. What is Exbridge's new business called?

16. When Qwill agrees to let Mrs. Young do his chart, what name does he use?

17. Who admits to Qwill that he is an ailurophobe?

18. What does Koko do that causes Kirt Nightingale to exit Qwill's apartment quickly?

19. After Qwill reads the editorial written by Don Exbridge, what does Koko do?

20. What does Koko do to predict the explosion at Edd's Editions?

21. Who is Winston?

22. How many versions of the robin painting that Qwill hung over his mantel did Misty paint?

23. What did Polly think of Qwill's *Two Robins with Worm* painting?

24. With whom does Maggie Sprenkle disappear?

25. What does Misty Morghan reveal to Qwill about Mayor Blythe?

26. Which volunteer fireman was killed while reporting vandalism and trespassing?

27. What did Ernie Kemple want to do with the property where Otto's Tasty Eats was?

28. Who is Jeffa Young?

29. Whom did Don Exbridge blame for breaking up his marriage to Robyn?

30. What does Robin tell Qwill about the relationship between Exbridge, Zoller, and Young?

31. Once Koko tired of the crystal martini pitcher, the bowl of wooden apples, and the "sharp corners of the pyramid lampshade tilting it or twisting it," what did he become obsessed with?

32. What causes Qwill to measure the height and depth of the wooden glove box? What does he discover?

33. What does one of the cats do that helps Qwill figure out how to open the false bottom of the glove box?

34. As soon as Qwill manages to get the false bottom of the box open, what does he find?

35. What does Qwill learn from Kemple and Campbell about Exbridge's plans for Otto's old building?

36. Who relates the story about the Three Bad Apples to Qwill?

37. Who are the Three Bad Apples?

38. On what pretense does Qwill invite Kirt Nightingale to his apartment?

39. After Qwill relates to Nightingale that talk has it that Omblower is back in town and wanted on murder and arson charges, what does Nightingale pick up and throw at Qwill?

40. Who was arrested for running an illegal investment scheme, called a Ponzi scheme?

🐾 Chronological Order of Events
Arrange the following incidents in their order of occurrence.

_____ A gunman shoots Ralph Abbey after trying to burn down the Big B shafthouse.

_____ Polly reports that Kirt had a "terrible row with another man."

_____ After Koko's smoke-sniffing episode, there is a brushfire near the Big B Mine site.

_____ Polly gives Qwill a wooden glove box, a gift to her from Nightingale.

_____ Qwilleran buys _Mysteries of Egyptian Pyramids_ from Eddington Smith's bookstore.

_____ When Qwill returns home from his duty on Citizens' Fire Watch, he finds Koko, "lying on the mantel, exhausted," has had another catfit.

_____ Qwill discovers a false bottom in the wooden glove box.

_____ Qwill and the sheriff's department set up a trap to catch Kirt Nightingale.

_____ George Omblower, alias Kirt, is arrested when he tries to escape.

_____ When Kirt Nightingale visits Qwill, Koko knocks off of the balcony one of the potted geraniums.

_____ Koko knocks another potted geranium off the balcony while Qwill reads Don Exbridge's letter to the editor.

_____ Cass Young falls down the stone steps at the Curling Club and dies.

_____ Qwill finds a letter to Helen Omblower in the bottom of the glove box.

_____ Koko pushes the wooden bowl with the three apples off the coffee table onto the Danish rug.

_____ Maggie Sprenkle tells Qwill that Henry Zoller doesn't think Cass Young's death was an accident.

_____ Gregory Blythe is arrested for operating an illegal investment scheme.

_____ Exbridge is charged later as an "accomplice-before-the-fact."

_____ Eddington Smith's bookstore blows up. Winston escapes.

_____ Koko vomits on Qwill's book about Egypt.

_____ Koko and Yum Yum stage another catfit, this time as a prelude to the Big One.

🐾 Koko and Yum Yum

1. Which cat can tell when mail comes from people with dogs or cats?

2. Which cat is "as good as an electronic sensor"?

3. Which cat hoards shiny objects and paper from the wastebasket?

4. Which cat sees the "invisible, hears the inaudible, and smells the unsmellable"?

5. When the two cats puff up "to resemble two porcupines on stilts," what are they trying to tell Qwill?

6. Which cat never walks across an area rug, but rather takes the long way around it?

7. Koko has learned that newsprint tears better lengthwise or crosswise?

🐾 Women in Qwill's Life

1. What is the arrangement Qwill and Polly have about groceries?

2. There are some things Qwill admits he can't tell Polly. Name three of them.

3. Who would "find it suffocating to live with the appurtenances of the nineteenth century"?

4. Where did Polly get many of the antiques that decorate her home?

🐾 Qwill's Living Quarters

1. Which unit and cluster at Indian Village does Qwill occupy?

2. Who lives in Unit One? In Unit Two? And in Unit Three?

3. Who adds the decorator's touch to Qwill's condo at Indian Village?

4. What is there about the "lush Danish rya rug" that causes Fran to suggest that Qwill buy it?

Dining Out

1. Whose new Sunday brunch offers "anything you want, as long as it's eggs"?

2. Where is the Windy Cliff Vineyard?

3. What was the Nutcracker Inn before it was a country inn?

4. Match the food to the place it was served.

   a. The meeting of the literary club at the Palomino Paddock
   b. Dinner at Maggie's
   c. Dinner at the Mackintosh Room
   d. Dinner at Barry Morghan's
   e. Dinner at Polly's

   _____ "A ragout of last week's chicken soup and this weekend's cassoulet, with garlic croutons and a sprinkling of goat cheese"

   _____ Paella, a dish of "chicken, rice, shrimp, and the Spanish sausage called chorizo"

   _____ Scotch eggs, grilled salmon, and blackberry cobbler

   _____ "Lobster bisque, filet of beef with sauced broccoli, a tossed green salad, and a white chocolate mousse"

   _____ "Medallions of beef and strawberries with peppercorn sauce"

5. Who cooked and served the dinner at Maggie's?

Crimes and Victims

1. How long had Kirt Nightingale been gone from Pickax?

2. Why was the mayor arrested?

3. Who exposed the corruption going on in Pickax?

4. Who killed Ralph (Ruff) Abbey and Cass Young?

5. What did Exbridge want the mine sites for?

THE CAT WHO
WENT UP THE
CREEK

General Questions

1. Why has Qwill agreed to spend some time at Nutcracker Inn?

2. Where is Polly going on vacation?

3. Which chapter from his collection of Moose County legends, some-day to be titled *Short & Tall Tales*, did Qwill read before heading off for Nutcracker Inn?

4. What does Nick Bamba discover behind the locked door leading to the turret?

5. What is visible in the window in the photo of the black walnut stair-case Qwill selects for publication in the *Moose County Something*?

6. Who invites Qwill to the MCCC luncheon?

7. From whose cabin does Qwill phone 911?

8. To what does Qwill attribute the house's bad vibes?

9. What is the name of the guest in Cabin Number Five?

10. Which book from the Limburger library does Qwill borrow to read to the cats?

11. What is Mrs. Hawley's hobby?

12. Mrs. Hawley is singing the role of Ruth in what play?

13. When Qwill, Koko, and Nick inspected Hackett's cabin, what two objects was Koko drawn to?

14. What physical characteristic does Nick remember seeing on Mr. Hackett?

15. Doyle Underhill likes the name of the *Moose County Something*, while his wife prefers its slogan, which is?

16. What is Doyle's profession?

17. What is Fran Brodie's mother's name?

18. What was Qwill's room number in the Nutcracker Inn? (This was before he moved to Cabin Number Five.)

19. What was on the front of Polly's first postcard to Qwill?

20. Who offers samples of his/her work to use as illustrations in Qwill's forthcoming book, *Short & Tall Tales*?

21. What book does Qwill borrow from Dr. Abernethy?

22. After Qwill moves into Cabin Five, what does he discover Koko has stashed from their earlier visit to the cabin?

23. What interrupted Qwill's dinner with Roger MacGillivray?

24. Which shoe, of the pair of oxford shoes Koko pilfered, interested him?

25. What is the name of the couple in Cabin Two?

26. According to Thornton Haggis, where might one go in years past to pan for gold?

27. Where did everyone believe the three veins of gold ran?

28. When Qwill returns from the presentation of *The Pirates of Penzance*, what does he find Koko has pushed off the shelf over the sofa?

29. Qwill encounters two obstacles on County 1124 as he bikes through the Black Forest Conservancy. What are they?

30. What are the three conservancies supported by the K Foundation?

31. Where will the black walnut furniture go on loan-exhibit?

32. Qwill proposes to Bart that the K fund publish a book of photography by Bushy and Doyle Underhill. What is the proposed book's title?

33. When Qwill returns to Cabin Five after talking to Hannah about Wendy's condition at the hospital, what is Koko keeping watch over?

34. What does Hannah confide to Qwill concerning her feelings about Joe Thompson? Why does she feel this way?

35. The luncheon at the MCCC was not what Qwill anticipated. What was this meeting of the MCCC?

36. What is "The Wright Brothers Special"?

37. Qwill remembers Koko calling his attention to a noisy truck. Whose truck was this, and what was coincidental about the truck and the gunshots Qwill heard while talking to Wendy?

38. Who was the girl that jumped off the Old Stone Bridge?

39. What did Qwill find and buy at an antique booth in Antique Village while attending Scottish Night?

40. When Qwill returns home from Scottish Night celebrations, what has Koko done with Doyle's photographs?

41. When Qwill shows the picnic photo to Jake Olsen, Jake identifies Joe Thompson. What else does Jake tell Qwill about Joe?

42. Koko had damaged only two of the photos selected by Qwill for the book. After Qwill studied the photo of the skunk "that Doyle had found comic," what did Qwill identify in the photo?

43. What is in the background of the photo of the squirrels?

44. What did the cats do to the moustache cup?

Chronological Order of Events

Arrange the following events in their order of occurrence.

_____ Qwill bikes in the Black Forest Conservancy and encounters a moving truck and its driver.

_____ Wendy is worried about Qwill, and while talking to Qwill, they hear gunshots in the distance.

_____ Polly asks Qwill about his vacation at the Nutcracker Inn.

_____ Qwill sorts through Doyle's photos and finds one of a skunk sitting on a forklift.

_____ Koko guards the video of *The Pirates of Penzance* and a novel by Trollope.

_____ Koko finds a pair of shoes under the bunk in Cabin Five.

_____ Nick, Qwill, and Koko check things out in Cabin Five. Koko is attracted to a pair of oxford shoes and a denture box.

_____ Qwill takes Koko for a walk down to the creek. They discover a body drifting down the creek.

_____ The sheriff's department asks for help in identifying a drowned man who wears dentures and has a birthmark under his left ear.

_____ Qwill discovers gold nuggets in the left heel of the shoe found in Cabin Five.

_____ The sheriff's department finds Doyle's body.

_____ An unidentified woman jumps off the Old Stone Bridge and drowns in Black Creek.

_____ The sheriff identifies the drowned woman as Marge Thompson.

_____ Qwill suspects that Joe Thompson left town after killing Doyle.

_____ Qwill shows Chief Brodie the two photos that Koko licked.

_____ Qwill walks around the barn two times, wondering how much of Koko's involvement was ESP and how much was coincidence.

🐾 Koko and Yum Yum

1. When Qwill and the cats move into their room at the Nutcracker Inn, what does Koko do immediately?

2. Which cat alerts Qwill when someone is approaching?

3. What do Koko and Yum Yum do prior to leaving Cabin Five?

4. Which cat bites Qwill's nose in order to wake him?

🐾 Women in Qwill's Life

1. Polly took Qwill up on his suggestion that "the picture on the front is less important than the message on the back" and sent several postcards this time. Arrange in their proper order the messages from Polly to Qwill.

   _____ Polly sees the Henry Ford Museum from a wheelchair.

   _____ Polly wishes Qwill could meet Walter.

   _____ Polly tells Qwill her luggage was lost, and Mona went to the hospital with "rhinitis."

   _____ Walter introduces Polly to Navy Grog, and she feels like dancing.

   _____ Polly tells Qwill that she met an "interesting antique dealer from Ohio."

   _____ Polly asks Qwill if he "could drop in and cheer the cats up."

   _____ Polly tells Qwill that she lost one of her earrings.

   _____ Polly tells Qwill that Walter found her earring.

2. Although the front of the postcard wasn't as important to Qwill as the message, can you put in order the places from which Polly sent postcards?

   _____ Mystic Seaport, Connecticut

_____ Sturbridge Village

_____ Airport Motel

_____ Colonial Williamsburg—British redcoats marching on Gloucester St.

_____ Governor's Palace at Williamsburg

_____ Early maritime village

_____ Henry Ford Museum

_____ Another view of Sturbridge Village

Qwill's Living Quarters

1. From what type of wood was the "circular staircase" from the third-floor bedroom to the turret carved?

2. What was added to the paint in order to give the walls of Nutcracker Inn a rich texture?

3. In which room of the cabin is there built-in seating?

4. Each of the cabins has a screened porch overlooking the creek. True or False?

5. Why were the old bedroom furniture pieces and cracked mirrors not removed when the Limburger mansion was liquidated?

Dining Out

1. What are the secret ingredients Nell Abernethy puts in her black walnut pie?

2. How does the Nasty Pasty prepare its crust and meat for a pasty?

3. Who eats what where? Match the meal to the person and the place where it is eaten.

   a. Visitors at the cabin celebrate the departure of Mrs. Truffle

   b. Qwill's first meal at the Nutcracker Inn

   c. Barb Ogilvie's dinner with Qwill at the Nutcracker Inn

   d. Dinner for Qwill at Arch and Mildred's

e. Meal at the Nutcracker Inn for the Underhills, Hannah, and Qwill in celebration of Hannah's success in *The Pirates of Penzance*

f. Arch and Mildred at Nutcracker Inn

_____ "Ramekin of corned beef hash with poached egg, served with black walnut muffins"

_____ "Cold puree of zucchini garnished with fresh blueberries" and beef pot pies

_____ Roast loin of lamb and lamb shank

_____ Grilled bacon-wrapped hot dogs and coleslaw

_____ Pork loin with quince and cinnamon glaze

_____ Leg of lamb and strawberry pie

Crimes and Victims

1. Why does Qwill believe Hackett was murdered?

2. Why does Qwill believe Doyle was murdered?

3. Who does Qwill suspect is the murderer of both Hackett and Doyle?

THE CAT WHO BROUGHT DOWN THE HOUSE

🐾 General Questions

1. Who has returned to Pickax after a long career in Hollywood?

2. What was the Opera House currently being used for?

3. Who said about crossbreeding man with cat, "It would improve the man but be deleterious to the cat?"

4. Qwill likes anything by Bizet. True or False?

5. Who is the county historian?

6. Who was Milo?

7. What were the names of Thelma's businesses that her father financed?

8. What was Thelma's brother's name? What did he do for a living?

9. Who gave Qwill the round silver tray?

10. What does Qwill suggest would happen if he didn't write his bimonthly column for the *Moose County Something*?

11. Who purchased the Old Stone Mill?

12. What will the new name of the Old Stone Mill be? Who will manage it?

13. What is the name of the new quilted art form?

14. Who was Mrs. Getz?

15. Who was elected general chairman of the Pickax Sesquicentennial celebration?

16. Who is Fran's new assistant?

17. Who is Fran's assistant's boyfriend?

18. Whose biography is Qwill reading to the cats now?

19. How old is Thelma Thackeray?

20. Who is Thelma's attorney?

21. In whose novels has there been a recent increase in interest at the Pickax Library?

22. In order to hide the nail holes in the wall above the fireplace, what does Qwill decide to do?

23. Who owns the land on which the houses on Pleasant Street reside?

24. How did Dr. Thurston supposedly die?

25. What was the new animal welfare project called?

26. Whose house did Thelma buy on Pleasant Street?

27. Where does Celia Robinson meet Qwill in order to exchange information?

28. How many parrots does Thelma have?

29. How does Thelma believe her father became wealthy?

30. What is Thelma's nephew's name?

31. Who is Janice?

32. Who was Thelma's cooking guru?

33. What was Thelma's "nouvelle approach, with accents on vegetables and fruits and seafood" called?

34. Who are Esmeralda, Pedro, Lolita, Carlotta, and Navarro?

35. Koko, Yum Yum, and Qwill finally settle on what book by Robert Louis Stevenson?

36. Who remembered seeing a delivery van behind the Thackeray house?

37. What happens to Thelma's parrots?

38. What were men carrying between vans when an occupant of a mobile home observed them from her home?

39. What happened after the men finished loading the boxes?

40. Who tells Qwill what Thelma's plans are for the old Opera House?

41. Who is Mr. Simmons?

42. Which parrot has "a large repertory of patriotic songs"? Which one "can recite the Greek alphabet"? Which one does "a perfect wolf-whistle"?

43. Which historical novel about the American Revolution did Koko knock off the shelf?

44. Who will be managing "Thelma's Film Club"?

45. From which book is Koko constantly encouraging Qwill to read?

46. Whom does Qwill ask to manage the bookstore if the K fund opened it?

47. What gift does Thelma send to Qwill? Who delivers it to the barn?

48. To whom did Thelma leave her estate?

49. What was the ransom exchanged for the return of Thelma's parrots?

50. What happened to Thelma's hat collection?

51. What was Richard using the Film Club for?

52. Did Thelma have a chance to draft and sign a new will?

53. What was Thelma's last message to Qwill?

🐾 Chronological Order of Events

Arrange the following events in their order of occurrence.

_____ Mildred Riker tells Qwill about the legend of the blueberries.

_____ Qwill holds a reception for Thelma.

_____ Mr. Simmons arrives from California.

_____ Qwill asks to write a column on the parrots, but Thelma says no—"The cocky little devils have had all the publicity they deserve."

_____ Thelma Thackeray dies peacefully in her sleep.

_____ Bushy photographs Thelma's hat collection.

_____ Thelma Thackeray, 82, a native of Moose County, retires and returns to Moose County.

_____ While listening to the radio, Qwill hears that an unidentified male has been shot to death at the wheel of a rented van.

_____ Burgess tells Qwill how Pleasant Street got its name.

_____ Jesse calls to tell Qwill that there's "something wrong with Thelma."

_____ Thelma discovers the missing inscribed sterling tray in Dick's office.

_____ Qwill discovers that the last letter written to Thelma by her brother is missing from the letter collection.

_____ Supporters of the Kit Kat Agenda attend a preview of the renovated Opera House.

_____ Qwill discovers a discrepancy between what Dick told the police about his father's death and what his father wrote in his last letter to Thelma.

_____ Qwill drives Thelma to Hilltop Cemetery so that she can spend a few moments at her father's grave.

_____ Qwill tells Polly that the house that Thelma bought is the one that she inherited.

_____ According to Thelma, her father invented the low-calorie potato chip.

_____ Polly tells Qwill that she is thinking about leaving the library, but she doesn't know what she will do.

_____ Koko knocks *Richard Carvel*, a historical novel by Winston Churchill, from the bookshelves.

_____ Celia tells Qwill that her husband Pat saw a delivery van drive around to the back of the Thackeray house.

_____ Janice tells Qwill that the parrots were kidnapped, and there was a ransom note, but that instead of telling the police, Dick took care of it. The parrots were returned.

_____ Koko knocks *A Child's Garden of Verses, The Strange Case of Dr. Jekyll and Mr. Hyde,* and *Travels with a Donkey* from the bookshelves.

Koko and Yum Yum
1. Which cat is "possessive about Qwilleran"?

2. Why does Qwill not think that Koko would eat food dispensed from an automatic feeder?

3. Who sent Qwill the "sterling silver thimble for the cats to play with"?

4. Which cat "considers it an invasion of privacy" to pose for a photo?

5. Why did Koko not take the sedative before the Kit Kat Revue?

Women in Qwill's Life
1. What does Qwill dislike about Fran?

2. Who thinks Fran's "kicking off her shoes when offered a second drink" is "just too cute"?

🐾 Qwill's Living Quarters

1. Where has Qwill put "adjustable bookshelves"?

2. What does Fran suggest that she get for Qwill to put up above the fireplace in place of the bookshelves?

3. Who made the "hand-crafted, custom-ordered" table with "hand-carved dovetailing in the drawers" that is in Qwill's foyer?

🐾 Dining Out

1. Who is the chef at the Grist Mill?

2. Who ordered what? Match the food to the person who ordered it.

   a. Qwill   b. Polly   c. Arch   d. Mildred

   _____ "Grilled venison tenderloin with smoked bacon, braised cabbage strudel and Bing cherry demi-glaze"

   _____ "Seafood Napoleon with carrot gaufrettes and lemon beurre blanc sauce"

   _____ "Garlic-and-black-pepper marinated strip loin with caramelized onions and merlot-vinegar reduction"

   _____ Blueberry cobbler

3. With whom does Qwill enjoy a French dip sandwich and a Caesar salad? Where were they eating?

4. What is a Qwilleran cocktail?

5. With whom and where does Qwill enjoy "a simple Chateaubriand, a twice-baked potato . . . broccoli . . . [and] blueberry cobbler?"

🐾 Crimes and Victims

1. Who is the first victim and what happens to him?

2. What is the inconsistency between what Richard told the police and what Bud wrote to his sister in his last letter to her?

3. How do we know that Thelma killed Richard?

4. What else do we learn from the tape recording?

CHARACTER IDENTIFICATION V

Who is who? Can you identify the following characters?

1. He is Fran Brodie's installer and referred to as Ruff. He was the Citizens' Fire Watch volunteer who was shot while reporting trespassing and vandalism.

2. The lawyer who joins the Hasselrich, Bennett and Barter law firm.

3. Pediatrician in Black Creek who shares his "The Little Old Man in the Woods" with Qwill.

4. Winston the cat's new family.

5. Wetherby Goode's cousin who is a corvidologist.

6. A twenty-five-year-old, woodsman by trade, student at MCCC who works as a desk clerk at the Mackintosh Inn. He wins the caber toss at the Highland Games.

7. A.k.a. Old Campo.

8. Don Exbridge's second wife who lives with Cass Young.

9. He teaches at Branchwater University and spent some time in Japan

before returning to Pickax in time to bid on the Danish rya rug at the Silent Auction.

10. Scottish architect who sported a flowing moustache.

11. Manager of the Mackintosh Inn.

12. A middle-aged rare book dealer who moves to Pickax and plans to publish his own rare book catalog and do mail-order business from his condo.

13. Her family owned the whole block across the street from the Mackintosh Inn.

14. A retired accountant whose hobby is "serious astrology."

15. A commercial fisherman from whom Qwill buys a handcrafted copper sailboat.

CLUES, CLUES, CLUES V

Can you identify the mystery based on the list of clues provided?

1. Silver tray
   Novels by William Makepeace Thackeray
   Poor Richard's Almanac
   Tape recorder
   The Gambler
   Robert Louis Stevenson novels

   _____

2. Missing backpacker
   A Horse's Tail
   Cabin cruiser
   Oedipus Rex
   Drug ring
   Potato skewer

   _____

3. Birthmark
   Shoes

The Pirates of Penzance
Black Forest Conservancy
Black Walnut
Gold nuggets

_____

4. Wildfires
Mysteries of Egyptian Pyramids
Bookstore explosion
Red apples
Glove box

_____

5. *Night Must Fall*
Jewelry
Bed pillow
"Collection" of pennies
Oedipus Rex
Towels

_____

PLACES, PLACES, PLACES V

How many places do you remember from your reading? See how many you can identify.

1. New film theater club opened by Thelma Thackeray.

2. What is the name of the new restaurant opened by Bushy's ex-wife?

3. What is the name of the restaurant opened by Elizabeth Cage?

4. A new retirement village near Kennebeck.

5. Lockmaster company that buys Mrs. Coggin's land.

6. New publishing house that will publish only ridiculous titles, e.g., *The Complete Works of Shakespeare in One Volume*.

7. A "first-class antique mall" in Black Creek. Owned by Ernie Kemple and Anne Munroe.

8. Commercial fishing business that shipped dried salted herring Down Below.

9. New enterprise created by Don Exbridge.

10. Motel on the Pickax medical campus that caters to families of patients.

11. What is Arch Riker's previous wife's antique shop called?

12. What is the name of the dining room at the Mackintosh Inn?

13. This business features the Oak Room for dogs, the Oyster Bar for cats, and the Palm Court for exercise. It's operated by Lori Bamba.

14. A new restaurant across from the Great Dune Motel.

15. The clubhouse resembles a Swiss chalet, and you go here to play a sport with stones and brooms on ice.

QWILL QUIZ V

What new things have you learned about Qwill? Take this quiz and find out.

1. When people in Moose County mention Qwill's "virtual landmark," to what are they referring?

2. What journalist from the eighteenth century does Qwill enjoy reading?

3. What was the most thoughtful explanation to the "Why do your cats squeeze their eyes?" question, the results of which Qwill used in a column?

4. What column does Qwill write in which he comments on grammatical errors made by Moose Countians?

5. When Qwill dresses up as a security guard so he can attend the tea given by Delacamp, what name does he use?

6. Qwill once wrote a column about the advantages and disadvantages of indoor plumbing. True or False?

7. Qwill once wrote a column on prevarications of all kinds. True or False?

8. At what time was Qwill born?

9. Who suggests that Qwill write an advice column called "Q-Tips"?

10. Qwill writes a column twice weekly. Arrange the following column topics in their order of appearance in the *Moose County Something*:

_____ Squirrels

_____ Misty Morghan's batiks

_____ Fourth of July from the view of Benjamin Franklin

_____ Dogcart races

_____ Blessing of the fishing fleet in the spring

_____ In praise of September

_____ Pet Plaza

_____ Hats

VICTIMS

1. Who was the first to die in a *Cat Who . . .* mystery?

2. Who was the first female to die in a *Cat Who . . .* mystery? (Hint: Not by suicide but by murder.)

3. Who was the first couple to die in a *Cat Who . . .* mystery? Who was the second couple?

4. What mother and son died in a *Cat Who . . .* mystery?

5. What father and son died in a *Cat Who . . .* mystery?

6. What father and daughter died in a *Cat Who . . .* mystery?

7. What aunt and nephew died in a *Cat Who . . .* mystery?

8. Can you arrange the following victims in the order of their demise in the series?

    _____ Andrew Glanz
    _____ Victor Greer
    _____ Irma Hasselrich
    _____ J. J. Hawkinfield
    _____ Lynette Duncan
    _____ Melinda Goodwinter

_____ C. C. Cobb
_____ Fanny Klingenschoen
_____ Iris Cobb
_____ Mrs. Coggin
_____ Earl Lambreth
_____ Dianne Bessinger
_____ Thelma Thackeray
_____ George Bonifield Mountclemens III
_____ George duLac

SHORT & TALL
TALES

A. Can you identify the legend from the clues?

    1. A giant tree with spreading roots
       Science fiction magazine
       Pears
       Small man
       Trees
       Woodcarvings
       A wood spirit

    _____

    2. Little green twigs
       Ax
       Drainage ditch
       Pipe
       Minerals

    _____

    3. One-room schoolhouse
       Snow

White face
Black garments

_____

4. Feed and seed dealer
   Brrr township
   Antique shops
   Scamadiddle

_____

5. Campbell graveyard
   Purple Point
   Diaries
   UFOs or "visitors"
   Tornado

_____

6. South edge of Pickax
   Carpenter Gothic
   Victorian colors
   "Wedding cake"

_____

7. Thirty-two miners
   Ephraim Goodwinter
   The undertaker's confession
   Bull moose
   Pickax Public Library

_____

8. Roebuck Magley
   "Bad air"
   Lunch pasties
   Arsenic
   Dr. Penfield

9. Commercial fishing
   Fishing nets
   Village of Fishport
   Silver disc with portholes
   Sightings every seven years

10. Wesley Prescott
    White Wing
    A shortcut home
    Swampland
    Apparition
    Broken nose
    Groceries

11. Siamese cat
    Luncheon
    Vicarage
    Bloody Mary

12. Ben Dibble
    Uncle
    Lightning
    Cases of booze
    Rumrunners
    Stonecutter

B. Can you identify the person Qwill interviewed for each of the following stories?

a. Reverend Arledge Harding
b. John Bushy
c. Burgess Campbell
d. Mildred Riker
e. Lisa Compton
f. Ozzie Penn
g. Gary Pratt

h. Thorton Haggis
i. Emma Wimsey
j. Silas Dingwell
k. Dr. Teresa Bunker
l. Roger MacGillivray
m. Maggie Sprenkle
n. Dr. Bruce Abernethy

_____ "Hilda the Clipper"
_____ "Milo the Potato Farmer"
_____ "The Little Old Man in the Woods"
_____ "My Great-Grandmother's Coal Mine"
_____ "Whooping It Up with the Loggers"
_____ " 'The Princess' and the Pirates"
_____ "The Scratching Under the Door"
_____ "The Mystery of Dank Hollow"
_____ "The Curious Fate of the *Jenny Lee*"
_____ "A Cat Tale: Holy Terror and the Bishop"
_____ "Those Pushy Moose County Blueberries"
_____ "Matilda, a Family Heroine"
_____ " 'Wild Cattin' with an Old Hog"
_____ "How Pleasant Street Got Its Name"

THE CAT WHO . . .
FOREIGN EDITIONS

1. Which four *Cat Who . . .* novels were only published in paperback?

2. Which book in the series has not been published in a United Kingdom edition?

3. What is Yum Yum called in the French versions?

4. What was the first book released in the Japanese series?

5. In what country is the *Daily Fluxion* referred to as the *Daily Fraction*?

6. In which country do *Cat Who . . .* fans read about Jim Kviller?

7. There have been several foreign editions of *The Cat Who . . .* novels. The most striking difference is typically that the order of publication is different than in the United States. Can you match the book title to the nationality of release?

   a. German b. Dutch c. French d. Japanese e. Spanish

   _____ *De Kat die een Spook Zag*
   _____ *Le Chat qui Mangeait Laine*
   _____ *Die Katze, die Rosa Pillen Nahm*
   _____ *Neko was Sheikusupea o Shitte Iru*
   _____ *El Gato que Odiaba el Rojo*

ANSWER KEY

THE EASY ONES!

1. Lilian Jackson Braun
2. James Mackintosh Qwilleran
3. *The Cat Who Could Read Backwards*
4. *The Cat Who Brought Down the House*
5. *The Cat Who Turned On and Off*
6. *The Cat Who Ate Danish Modern*
7. 3,000
8. It's "four hundred miles north of everywhere."
9. *Moose County Something*
10. She is head librarian
11. Kabibbles
12. Klingenschoen Foundation/K fund
13. Lanspeak Department Store
14. 315 Park Circle
15. *Pickax Picayune*
16. One of Polly's cats
17. Kao K'o-Kung
18. Hasselrich, Bennett and Barter
19. Lois's Luncheonette
20. Ittibittiwassee River
21. "The Sin of Madame Phloi"
22. *Detroit Free Press*
23. *Fiat Flux*

24. Squunk water
25. *Short & Tall Tales*

IN THE BEGINNING . . .
1. *The Cat Who Wasn't There*
2. *The Cat Who Robbed a Bank*
3. *The Cat Who Moved a Mountain*
4. *The Cat Who Sang for the Birds*
5. *The Cat Who Tailed a Thief*
6. *The Cat Who Saw Stars*
7. *The Cat Who Went Into the Closet*
8. *The Cat Who Could Read Backwards*
9. *The Cat Who Said Cheese*
10. *The Cat Who Knew a Cardinal*
11. *The Cat Who Lived High*
12. *The Cat Who Smelled a Rat*
13. *The Cat Who Came to Breakfast*
14. *The Cat Who Saw Red*
15. *The Cat Who Turned On and Off*

QUICK ASSOCIATIONS
1. *The Cat Who Saw Stars*
2. *The Cat Who Blew the Whistle*
3. *The Cat Who Robbed a Bank*
4. *The Cat Who Ate Danish Modern*
5. *The Cat Who Played Brahms*
6. *The Cat Who Saw Red*
7. *The Cat Who Could Read Backwards*
8. *The Cat Who Said Cheese*
9. *The Cat Who Knew Shakespeare*
10. *The Cat Who Went Into the Closet*
11. *The Cat Who Played Post Office*
12. *The Cat Who Turned On and Off*
13. *The Cat Who Went Underground*
14. *The Cat Who Talked to Ghosts*
15. *The Cat Who Wasn't There*
16. *The Cat Who Lived High*
17. *The Cat Who Sniffed Glue*
18. *The Cat Who Moved a Mountain*
19. *The Cat Who Knew a Cardinal*
20. *The Cat Who Smelled a Rat*

THE CAT WHO COULD READ BACKWARDS
General Questions
1. In an old, cheap hotel
2. 427,463
3. *Fiat Flux*
4. In Mountclemens's apartment
5. Thirteenth-century artist of Turkish descent who lived in China

Chronological Order of Events
3, 1, 2, 6, 4, 5, 7, 8, 9, 10

Koko
1. True
2. True
3. False
4. True

Women in Qwill's Life
1. Sandra Halapay, a.k.a. Sandy
2. Zoe Lambreth

Qwill's Living Quarters
1. The low level of lighting
2. Monet

Dining Out
1. c 2. b 3. a

Crimes and Victims
1. Mountclemens
2. Narx
3. Stabbed in the throat with a chisel

THE CAT WHO ATE DANISH MODERN
General Questions
1. *Gracious Abodes*
2. Draperies/drapes
3. White
4. Villa Verandah
5. 15F
6. Bald, sacroiliac, rubeola, koolokamba
7. Thorvaldson

Chronological Order of Events
2, 5, 3, 6, 4, 8, 7, 9, 10, 1

Koko and Yum Yum
1. True
2. True
3. Freya
4. Yu
5. K, Y, Y, Y, K

Women in Qwill's Life
1. Fran Unger, women's editor
2. 5, 2, 1, 3, 4
3. Al

Qwill's Living Quarters
1. Architect's Revenge
2. 18
3. Harry Noyton
4. Scandihoovian

Dining Out
1. Caviar, shrimp, rarebit, mushrooms, meatballs, artichoke hearts, dill sauce
2. Cream, ginger ale, and nutmeg

Crimes and Victims
1. Natalie Noyton.
2. A bullet in the chest.
3. She commits suicide with a combination of alcohol and pills.

THE CAT WHO TURNED ON AND OFF
General Questions
1. Medford Manor.
2. 606.
3. $3,000 in cash prizes and twenty-five frozen turkeys for honorable mention.
4. The Mackintosh Coat of Arms.
5. C. C. Cobb.
6. Duxbury.
7. Money.
8. They went into antique shops and asked for horse brasses.
9. "The ubiquitous E."

Chronological Order of Events
4, 3, 10, 1, 2, 5, 6, 7, 8, 9, 11, 12

Koko and Yum Yum
1. In the springs of Qwill's bed
2. By playing hopscotch on the bed
3. On the left

Women in Qwill's Life
1. From his mother-in-law, Miriam's mother
2. From Cokey, canceling their date for Christmas Eve
3. C, MD, MD, MD, C

Qwill's Living Quarters
1. Medicare Manor.
2. To The Junkery, owned by the Cobbs.
3. MM, TJ, MM, TJ, TJ, TJ, MM
4. William Towne Spencer, in 1855.
5. Spencer was an abolitionist, and the passageway was used as an Underground Railroad.
6. Mathilda.

Dining Out
1. Cranberry juice cocktail, piroshki, pot roast, mashed potatoes, salad with Roquefort dressing, coconut cake
2. "A bowl of chowder . . . and some cheese and crackers"
3. True
4. "Oysters Rockefeller and pressed duck and Chateaubriand and French strawberries"
5. A case of canned lobster

Crimes and Victims
1. Ben Nicholas killed Glanz; Glanz knew Ben was dealing drugs, and Ben was afraid Glanz would turn him in.
2. Ben also killed Cobb because Cobb was blackmailing Ben because he, too, knew that Ben was dealing in heroin.
3. No.

THE CAT WHO SAW RED
General Questions
1. 30
2. Bourbon
3. 4, 2, 1, 3, 5
4. H. M. H., Helen Maude Hake
5. "Prandial Musings"

Chronological Order of Events
1, 5, 2, 14, 13, 15, 17, 6, 7, 8, 9, 11, 18, 12, 10, 3, 4, 16

Koko and Yum Yum
1. Stepping on the tab key of the typewriter
2. Lobster, chicken, beef

Women in Qwill's Life
1. True
2. To San Francisco
3. $750
4. Rosemary Whiting
5. R, R, J, J, R, J

Qwill's Living Quarters
1. Number 6.
2. River Road.
3. False.
4. It was an art center called Penniman Plaza.

Dining Out
1. Toledo Tombs
2. The Golden Lamb Chop/vichyssoise, rack of lamb, herring in sour cream, banana Bavarian
3. MH, PB, TT, RI, FF, FF, MH
4. S, R, CR, MM, HR

Crimes and Victims
1. She was cremated in the kiln.
2. Her husband, Dan Graham, killed her because he wanted credit for her color glazes.
3. Dan Graham spiked William's drink with lead oxide.

THE CAT WHO PLAYED BRAHMS
General Questions
1. Green/He was measuring to see if there was sufficient space for the cats' commode.
2. No later than September 1.
3. Ninety.
4. Investigative reporting.
5. He will get hives.
6. Aunt Fanny.
7. Four/three envelopes, "sealed with red wax and labeled 'Last Will and Testament.' The fourth item was a small address book."
8. He has to live in Pickax for five years.
9. Second, oldest, final.

Chronological Order of Events
8, 5, 4, 1, 2, 6, 3, 7, 10, 9, 11, 14, 15, 12, 13

Koko and Yum Yum
1. Yum Yum
2. Koko
3. Yum Yum
4. K, Y
5. Koko
6. Koko

Women in Qwill's Life
1. Rosemary and Melinda Goodwinter
2. Melinda Goodwinter
3. Rosemary

4. Rosemary
5. Check all the statements except for "She wasn't attractive and compassionate."

Qwill's Living Quarters
1. English pub, Georgian silver, Staffordshire collection, paneled library, grand staircase
2. Moose head, screened porches, fieldstone chimney, whirlpool bath, exposed logs

Dining Out
1. Northern Lights Hotel
2. FOO
3. Dimsdale Diner
4. Old Stone Mill
5. Northern Lights Hotel
6. Nasty Pasty
7. "Mediocre pork chops, a soggy baked potato, and overcooked green beans"

Crimes and Victims
1. Stanley Hanstable/a big candlestick that Buck made.
2. His odor, the scratches on his face, his torn ear, and Qwill recognizes his voice as the one on the tape.
3. Inside the turkeys he delivered to the prison.
4. Buck learned about Hanstable's involvement in the "ferry racket."
5. Hanstable smuggled men from the prison and dumped them into the lake.
6. He is disillusioned when he discovers that he isn't going to get any money from Fanny and can't buy his nightclub.

CHARACTER IDENTIFICATION I
1. Mrs. Allison
2. Mr. Anderson
3. Cluthra, Amberina, and Ivrene
4. Mildred Hanstable
5. Alacoque Wright
6. Fran Unger
7. Nino, a.k.a. Joseph Hibber
8. Roger MacGillivray
9. David Lyke
10. "Dr." Highspight
11. Hames
12. Andrew Glanz
13. Mary Duckworth
14. C. C. Cobb
15. Percy/Harold Bates
16. Lodge Kendall
17. Robert Maus
18. Mrs. Marron
19. Rosemary Whiting
20. William Towne Spencer
21. Max Sorrel
22. Charlotte Roop
23. Rosie Riker
24. Oscar Narx
25. George Bonifield Mountclemens III
26. Mrs. McGuffey
27. George Verning Tait
28. Old Bunsen
29. Joy Wheatley Graham
30. Stanley Hanstable

CLUES, CLUES, CLUES I
1. *The Cat Who Ate Danish Modern*
2. *The Cat Who Could Read Backwards*
3. *The Cat Who Turned On and Off*
4. *The Cat Who Played Brahms*
5. *The Cat Who Saw Red*

PLACES, PLACES, PLACES I
1. Canard Street
2. Down Below
3. Moose County
4. Muggy Swamp
5. Toldeo Restaurant/Toledo Tombs
6. Lois's Luncheonette
7. FOO
8. Dimsdale Diner
9. Blue Dragon
10. The Junkery
11. Lambreth Gallery
12. Medford Manor
13. Villa Verandah
14. Northern Lights Hotel

QWILL QUIZ I
1. James Mackintosh Qwilleran.
2. 6 foot 2 inches.
3. March 24.
4. Chicago.
5. Jamesy.
6. Anne Mackintosh Qwilleran/Massachusetts.
7. Spenser's *Fairie Queene*.
8. Camp outs and cookouts.
9. Snoopy.
10. *North Wind*/editor.
11. An actor.
12. *The Mikado, Androcles and the Lion, The Glass Menagerie, The Frogs*.
13. True.
14. False. He met her in Scotland.
15. Miriam/about ten years.

THE CAT WHO HAD 14 TALES
A.
1. Phut Phat
2. Marmalade
3. Percy
4. Drooler
5. Sin-Sin
6. Dahk Won
7. Tipsy
8. Conscience/Constance
9. Stanley and Spook
10. SuSu
11. Stanley
12. Madame Phloi
13. Shadow
14. Whiskers

B.
1. Madame Phloi
2. Stanley and Spook
3. Shadow
4. Drooler
5. Marmalade
6. Sin-Sin
7. Tipsy
8. Conscience
9. SuSu
10. Percy

THE CAT WHO PLAYED POST OFFICE
General Questions
1. In the Pickax Hospital/He fell off his bicycle on Ittibittiwassee Road.
2. 20 years.
3. "Some outfit in New Jersey."
4. Four: "a white-haired woman," one who ran away after she saw the cats, Tiffany Trotter, and Mrs. Fulgrove.
5. Miners considered it bad luck to whistle in the mines, and now there is "no whistling in Pickax—by city ordinance."
6. "Only thirty miles."
7. Down Below.
8. He suggests that the council "preserve the present flag as a memorial to the donor and as a historic artifact, mounting it on the wall under glass" and "accept my gift of a new custom-made, all-wool, silk-lined, floor-standing flag."
9. Arch Riker.
10. Forty-two.

Chronological Order of Events
7, 2, 1, 3, 8, 4, 5, 6, 11, 9, 10, 14, 12, 13, 15

Koko and Yum Yum
1. Third step
2. Yum Yum
3. "Bicycle Built for Two," "Three Blind Mice," and "How Dry I Am"
4. Hixie Rice

Women in Qwill's Life
1. Penelope Goodwinter
2. 3, 1, 2
3. P, M, P, M, P, M

Qwill's Living Quarters
1. 80.
2. Alcatraz Provincial or the Bastille.
3. 16.

4. The breakfast room.
5. The library.
6. Two each.
7. F, E, OE, B
8. The walls and ceiling are "covered with graffiti in every color available in a spray can." Flowers that look like daisies on every surface and "initials, and references to LUV."

Dining Out
1. Hotel Booze Dining Room
2. Ravioli
3. Otto's Tasty Treats
4. Stephanie's/their cow
5. broccoli/the chef insisted that it was asparagus

The Klingenschoen Mansion Dinner Party
6. Terrine of pheasant, jellied watercress consomme, salmon croquettes, lamb Bucheronne with potatoes and mushrooms, asparagus vinaigrette and raspberry trifle

Crimes and Victims
1. A combination of alcohol and drugs.
2. She was buried alive at Three Pine Mine.
3. Birch Trevelyan, a.k.a. Birch Tree.
4. In a plane crash.

THE CAT WHO KNEW SHAKESPEARE
General Questions
1. November.
2. The Pennsylvania *Schrank* and Ephraim Goodwinter's old desk.
3. Old Stone Church, Little Stone Church, courthouse, and public library.
4. Ephraim Goodwinter, the founder of the library.
5. Herb Hackpole.
6. He was a firefighter, and he died in a barn fire.
7. A big white cat that is the official mouser at the *Pickax Picayune*.
8. Don Exbridge, Cass Young, and Dr. Zoller.
9. 4, 3, 1, 2, 5, 7, 6

Chronological Order of Events
1, 11, 2, 8, 7, 3, 4, 5, 6, 10, 9, 12, 13, 14, 15

Koko and Yum Yum
K, K, K, Y, K

Women in Qwill's Life
1. Pickax Public Library/She is the head librarian.
2. 25 years.
3. New England.
4. Literature.
5. He was a volunteer fireman and was killed fighting a fire years ago.
6. Hippolyta, the name of a character in *A Midsummer Night's Dream*.

Qwill's Living Quarters
1. To an apartment in the carriage house
2. Four: sitting room, writing studio, bedroom, and the cats' parlor

Dining Out
1. Polly
2. Hixie Rice
3. Tony Peters
4. Tony Peters's real name/the chef at the Old Stone Mill
5. Tony Peters/Antoine Delapierre
6. Polly

Crimes and Victims
1. "He rammed [his car] into the stone rail, flipped head over tail, landed on the rocks in the river. Car caught on fire."
2. "Ephraim *hanged* himself or so they said" and Zack Whittlestaff killed Titus with a hunting knife.
3. "Their car struck and killed a large buck, then entered a ditch and rolled over."
4. Herb Hackpole/He dies in the fire.
5. His car is stuck in a snowdrift.
6. Herb Hackpole/He does something to the car to make it "go out of control and burst into flames."
7. Basil Whittlestaff.

THE CAT WHO SNIFFED GLUE
General Questions
1. Drunk driving! Underage drinking! Vandalism!
2. Chad Lanspeak.
3. Eddington Smith's cat.
4. *Arsenic and Old Lace.*
5. She had her father, Chief Brodie, run a check on Qwill's driver's registration.
6. Snowshoes.
7. Arch Riker.
8. Harley Fitch and Wife Found Shot to Death/Burglary Obvious Motive.
9. "There's a deceitful woman involved!"

10. She reveals that Qwill's picture is a reproduction: "There are ten copies of this picture floating around the county. . . . The original is in the Fitch mansion."
11. *Fitch Witch*.
12. He was in prison, serving time for criminal negligence. He was involved in a car accident that killed a girl.
13. An early work on anatomy—a very rare book.
14. Each one "regularly worked with adhesives."
15. Qwill and Hixie Rice.

Chronological Order of Events
11, 12, 1, 13, 3, 4, 6, 5, 2, 8, 10, 7, 9

Koko and Yum Yum
1. "He tilted the gunboat picture that hung over the sofa" and sniffed *Moby-Dick, Captains Courageous, Two Years Before the Mast*, and *Mutiny on the Bounty*.
2. Biographies.
3. K, K, K, Y, K, Y, Y

Women in Qwill's Life
F, MC, P, P, P, P, F, F, MC, F

Qwill's Living Quarters
1. In the carriage-house apartment.
2. Francesca Brodie, assistant in Amanda Goodwinter's interior design studio.
3. "Oatmeal-colored, oatmeal-textured," hand-woven Scottish tweed.
4. One of "an 1805 gunboat that used to sail the Great Lakes."
5. She suggests "draped walls, fur bedcover, and mirrored ceilings."
6. Alacoque Wright.
7. 300.

Dining Out
1. Stephanie's.
2. Hotel Booze in Brrr.
3. Brrr/Polish.
4. Mrs. Cobb.
5. Tipsy's.
6. The cake was decorated with a bugle and the theater's traditional wish. "Break a leg, darling!"

Crimes and Victims
1. She has a stroke.
2. He commits suicide.

3. Belle.
4. He dies in a car-train accident. "Three youths . . . rammed their car into the side of a moving freight train."
5. "It started at [his] . . . birthday party . . . [when] Koko took an instant liking to Harley . . . and [again] at the Fitch library . . . Koko could smell the spirit gum! The moustache was false. . . ."
6. Jill.
7. Jill/to destroy the twins' dental records.

THE CAT WHO WENT UNDERGROUND
General Questions
1. Polly is going to be away for the summer./The refrigerator in his apartment is out of order./Pickax is boring during warm weather.
2. 2/"Straight from the Qwill Pen."
3. $300: "Two hun'erd to join. . . . Fifty a year dues, or a hun'erd if you wanna be on the fast track."
4. Top o' the Dunes Club.
5. She believes that "Shakespeare was really a woman."
6. True.
7. Blue.
8. e, a, b, c, d
9. The first, "take precautions . . . to protect your family," which Qwill interpreted to mean take care of the cats. The second was "about an excavation," which disturbed Qwill. The messages were sent to him by Joy.
10. *Say Cheese*.
11. A tornado hit the shore and destroyed the new addition.
12. Small.
13. He discovers while reading papers given to him by Mrs. Wimsey that she is Little Jo's grandmother.
14. Clem's.
15. He read a survey that horoscopes have a larger percentage of readers than anything else in the paper.

Chronological Order of Events
11, 1, 2, 4, 6, 3, 5, 8, 14, 12, 9, 7, 13, 15, 16, 17, 10

Koko and Yum Yum
1. First, the one on Switch, the electrician's dog, and then the one on Mrs. Wimsey's cat, Punkin
2. Yum Yum
3. Koko
4. Koko
5. Koko

Women in Qwill's Life

1. In England on an exchange program.
2. Her doctors advise her to do so because she has a "bad case of bronchitis and asthma."
3. Mildred Hanstable.
4. UFOs and horoscopes.

Qwill's Living Quarters

1. 75 years old
2. 100 miles
3. 1, 4, 9, 8, 2, 5, 6, 7, 3
4. 315 Park Circle

Dining Out

1. Clam chowder and boiled whitefish.
2. The Hot Spot/Specialties include Mexican, Cajun, and East Indian dishes.
3. Palomino Paddock.
4. Fried chicken, baked beans, Cornish pasties, ham sandwiches, deviled eggs, reunion potato salad, homemade freezer pickles, apple juice salad, Granny Wimsey's chocolate sheet cake, thimbleberry pie, molasses cookies.
5. Mildred Hanstable.

Crimes and Victims

1. Joe Trupp/Tailgate of a dump truck falls on him.
2. Mert.
3. He "drank himself to death, as everyone thought."
4. 2, 4, 1, 5, 3
5. "They're bad! . . . daddy was a carpenter! He was a bad man!"

THE CAT WHO TALKED TO GHOSTS
General Questions

1. Verdi's *Otello*.
2. Herb Hackpole.
3. Larry Lanspeak.
4. Dennis Hough.
5. Letters Mrs. Cobb wrote to her son.
6. 1904.
7. The Noble Sons of the Noose.
8. Bootsie.
9. The Pennsylvania German *Schrank* and her personal recipe books.
10. He goes to the office; he tries to reach Mrs. Finney's feather duster.
11. The exhibit of textiles.
12. She says she sees "her whenever there is a thunderstorm. . . . She walks upstairs in a flowing white robe . . . up into the tower—and then disappears."
13. Emmaline.

14. Breeds of goats raised by Kristi Fugtree Waffle.
15. A Bible.
16. Disasters in Moose County history.
17. "A ghoulish picture of the Hanging Tree with (presumbably) a body hanging from a rope."
18. *To Kill a Mockingbird* and *One Flew Over the Cuckoo's Nest*.
19. The "white sheet that the Reverend Mr. Crawbanks found near the Hanging Tree after Ephraim's death."
20. Iris's notebook of recipes.
21. Types of printing presses.
22. Buried under the house.
23. That "Ephraim weren't dead!" and that the Goodwinters paid hush money to Dingleberry's father so that there was nothing said about the death of Luther Bosworth.
24. ". . . no jewels . . . There were bills, receipts and promissory notes."
25. $3,000.
26. Verona Boswell or Whitmoor.
27. Boswell using a hammer to knock out the mortar.

Chronological Order of Events
1, 4, 2, 3, 7, 9, 12, 13, 10, 11, 14, 8, 5, 6, 15

Koko and Yum Yum
1. Koko.
2. Koko "laid his ears back."
3. These were indications of "how they might react to abandonment in a new environment."
4. Poultry.

Women in Qwill's Life
P, P, M, P, P, M

Qwill's Living Quarters
1. Black Creek Lane.
2. One dollar.
3. This was Qwill's wedding gift to Mrs. Cobb when she married Herb Hackpole.
4. He dreams that the headboard of the General Grant bed falls on him.
5. Correct statements are a, b, c, and e.

Dining Out
1. Broiled whitefish, Petite salad, French onion soup, frog legs, and pumpkin pecan pie.
2. Tipsy's/Tipsy's Tavern.

3. Indian cooking is her new specialty, with lots of hot curry.
4. Tipsy's Tavern.

Crimes and Victims
1. Vince Boswell.
2. She was smothered with a pillow.
3. Brent Waffle, her former husband.
4. Vince Boswell/"Hit on the head with a blunt instrument."

CHARACTER IDENTIFICATION II
1. John Bushland
2. Verona Whitmoor Boswell
3. Francesca/Fran Brodie
4. Buddy Yarrow
5. Emma Wimsey
6. Gary Pratt
7. Mrs. Fish-eye
8. Chief Andrew Brodie
9. Lyle Compton
10. Adam Dingleberry
11. Kevin Doone
12. Thelma
13. Wally Toddwhistle
14. Joe Trupp
15. Zack Whittlestaff
16. Eddington Smith
17. Russell Simms
18. Bruce Scott
19. Tony Peters, a.k.a. Antoine Delapierre
20. Mr. Pat O'Dell
21. Harry Noyton
22. Mitch Ogilvie
23. Mr. MacGregor
24. Larry Lanspeak
25. Dennis Hough

CLUES, CLUES, CLUES II
1. *The Cat Who Sniffed Glue*
2. *The Cat Who Talked to Ghosts*
3. *The Cat Who Went Underground*
4. *The Cat Who Played Post Office*
5. *The Cat Who Knew Shakespeare*

PLACES, PLACES, PLACES II
1. Black Bear Café
2. Zoller Clinic
3. XYZ Enterprises
4. North Pole Café
5. New Pickax Hotel
6. Moose County Historical Society
7. Lanspeak Department Store
8. Indian Village
9. Hasselrich, Bennett and Barter
10. Hotel Booze
11. Edd's Editions
12. Dingleberry Funeral Home
13. North Middle Hummock
14. Black Creek
15. Brrr
16. Chipmunk
17. Kennebeck
18. Lockmaster
19. Purple Point
20. Sawdust City

QWILL QUIZ II
1. Scotland.
2. Red or some shade of red.
3. Lori Bamba.
4. The weather, especially the Big One.
5. True.
6. Hixie Rice.
7. Eddington Smith, owner of Edd's Editions.
8. "Straight from the Qwill Pen."
9. He had never raked leaves.
10. He searches for the cats.

THE GOODS ON THE GOODWINTERS
1. Senior/Titus/Ephraim.
2. Dr. Halifax/Hal.
3. Jack/Los Angeles.
4. Pug/Montana.
5. Titus and Samson/Samson is the oldest.
6. Emory/He appears in Pickax under the name Charles Edward Martin.
7. Penelope and Alexander.
8. Ephraim.
9. Amanda.
10. Junior.
11. Titus Goodwinter.
12. Melinda.
13. Gage.
14. b, c, a, c, d/f, e
15. c, h, e, b, a, d, g, f

READ ALL ABOUT IT! NEWSPAPERS "400 MILES NORTH OF EVERYWHERE"
SG, DF, DF, PP, MCS, LL, LL, MR, DF, DF, MCS, MCS, MCS, MCS, PP, PP, PP

THE CAT WHO LIVED HIGH
General Questions
1. Save Our Casablanca Kommittee.
2. To "his place in Pickax."
3. Purple plum.
4. 14A, on the thirteenth floor.
5. Keestra Hedrog.
6. "A large dark stain . . . Blood!"
7. Dianne Bessinger/She was murdered.
8. "One night some kids—high on something—drove by and shot [him]."
9. Gateway Alcazar.

10. Penniman, Greystone and Fleudd.
11. 28.
12. "Table games—cards, Parcheesi, checkers, mah-jongg, anything except chess."
13. The "plastic pails standing around the living room to catch drips when the skylight leaks."
14. "One disc was engraved in cursive script: 'To Dianne' . . . Another was inscribed: 'From Ross.'"
15. Numerals, for example, "1-1-4-1, 5-1-1-1, 4-1-3-5, etc."
16. Three: Diane, Diana, Dianne.
17. True.
18. "A book about the historic Casablanca, using old photos from the public library."
19. Di Bessinger.
20. Boar, soar, hoar, and hoax.
21. Jack Yazbro/#18.
22. "The board voted unanimously to foot the bill for saving the Casablanca, leaving the amount entirely to Qwill's discretion."
23. "Lady Di signed herself D-I-a-n-n-e. . . . The Van Gogh was a gift from Ross, and he inscribed it 'To D-I-a-n-n-e from Ross.'" He also used two *n*s in the bracelet inscription, so why would he misspell the name on the wall?
24. Bartender at Penniman Plaza.
25. Vincent.
26. A knife.
27. Raymond Dunwoody.
28. True.

Chronological Order of Events

4, 10, 11, 5, 16, 9, 1, 13, 18, 2, 17, 6, 8, 3, 12, 7, 14, 15

Koko and Yum Yum

1. Yum Yum.
2. Yum Yum.
3. Chocolate and strawberry.
4. They burrow under rugs.

Women in Qwill's Life

1. Mrs. Tuttle
2. Mary Duckworth
3. Polly
4. Amberina/Amber
5. Winnie Wingfoot

Qwill's Living Quarters

1. 1901.
2. In Junktown.
3. White glazed brick in a "modified Moorish design."
4. A refrigerator; there is a "dark line across the façade at the ninth floor."

5. She lives on the twelfth floor.
6. Three: a red one, a green one, and the bronze elevator with scenes from *Don Quixote* and *Carmen*. The bronze elevator is a private one to the countess's floor.

Dining Out
a, c, d, b

Crimes and Victims
1. She was murdered. Her throat was cut.
2. An apparent suicide.
3. Raymond Dunwoody/It is assumed that he dies in the explosion at the Casablanca.
4. Rexwell Fleudd/Randy Jupiter/Raymond Dunwoody.

THE CAT WHO KNEW A CARDINAL
General Questions
1. Dennis Hough, Mrs. Cobb's son.
2. Horseface.
3. Fiona Stucker/Lockmaster.
4. *Henry VIII.*
5. VanBrook expelled him a week before graduation because of a prank.
6. Hixie Rice.
7. Lyle Compton, Mildred Hanstable, and Qwill.
8. He is collecting printing memorabilia.
9. He has gone back to St. Louis to see his family.
10. Hixie Rice.
11. "Don't come home, Dennis! Not ever! I've filed for divorce. I've found someone who'll be a good daddy for Denny and a real husband for me."
12. Suicide.
13. He requested $700 and paid her $200.
14. $50,000.
15. Son of Cardinal.
16. W. Chase Amberton.
17. *Stablechat.*
18. Typefaces.
19. Steve O'Hare, alias Redbeard.
20. She was his housekeeper.
21. Japanese.
22. It might be saffron.
23. The Pickax School System.
24. Money: ten- and twenty-dollar bills.
25. That the books in the boxes were leaved with counterfeit money.
26. Eddington Smith.

27. As he draws a gun, the apple tree textile falls on him.
28. He asked what happened to the trees in the orchard; if he hadn't been there before, he wouldn't have known anything was different. It looked like some work had been done to the right-hand side of his truck. There were two wills: "one dated recently, naming Pickax as the beneficiary, and a prior will naming Steve's stableboy as the sole heir."

Chronological Order of Events
2, 4, 1, 13, 14, 5, 8, 7, 3, 6, 9, 10, 11, 12, 15, 16

Koko and Yum Yum
1. Yum Yum.
2. At the house they try to get in every picture. At his studio they refuse to get out of their carrier.
3. They were "unimpressed."

Women in Qwill's Life
P, M, M, P, S, S, P, P, S

Qwill's Living Quarters
1. J. Mayfus & Son
2. 1881
3. True
4. Three
5. A contemporary fireplace
6. The first balcony
7. The second one
8. The top or third one
9. b, a

Dining Out
1. Dry sherry
2. Tipsy's Tavern
3. Lois's Luncheonette in Pickax
4. Qwill

Crimes and Victims
1. Steve O'Hare.
2. He was despondent after the message his wife left him telling him not to come home and that she had found another man.

THE CAT WHO MOVED A MOUNTAIN
General Questions
1. The east side.
2. Yellohoo.
3. $1.2 million.
4. Manager of the market at Five Points.
5. "Potato Peelings."
6. Qwill.
7. True.

8. A gazebo.
9. T, NT
10. True.
11. "In his fifties."
12. "She was committed to a mental hospital, and she's still there. . . ."
13. He buys jackets for "Polly, Mildred, Fran, Lori, and Hixie."/$100 each.
14. Forest Beechum.
15. "The two younger boys were buried in an avalanche while skiing, and the older boy was lost in the river."
16. "She made a vow never to speak another word as long as he's [Forest] in prison."
17. Some of the Beechum kinfolk go to the "top of Little Potato at midnight, carrying lanterns. They walk in a silent circle and meditate, concentrating on getting Forest released."
18. No.
19. Bill Treacle.
20. He found out that she was dating a Lumpton.
21. He says he is planning to write a book about J. J. Hawkinfield.
22. An illegal fund that purportedly supported the local economy while in actuality was financing the illegal distilling and hauling of bootlegged whisky to consumers.
23. He thought she was the most likely person to know that her father was about to release an editorial that would have suggested Josh Lumpton was involved in the Hot Potato Fund. Her false testimony at the trial suggested also that she was trying to protect both her father-in-law and her future husband.
24. Ones on crime.
25. It is "a handful of ash-blond hair mixed with lint and dust."
26. Qwill sees "Hugh as the mastermind of the Hot Potato Fund. . . . Josh was the organizer of the bootleg operation. . . . Hugh's future wife [Sherry] collaborated because she wanted to inherit her father's estate."

Chronological Order of Events
15, 11, 16, 6, 5, 9, 4, 1, 13, 10, 14, 2, 8, 3, 7, 12

Koko and Yum Yum
1. K, Y
2. He uses the "T-word: Treat!"
3. He stands on his hind paws behind the steering wheel and puts a forepaw on the horn button.
4. Yum Yum.
5. One of mountains, painted by Forest Beechum.
6. Koko.
7. The cats have managed to raise the bedroom window shades.

Women in Qwill's Life
1. Melinda Goodwinter
2. Polly
3. Vonda Dudley Wix/Cookie
4. e, c, a, b, d

Qwill's Living Quarters
1. "Musty Rustic"
2. 1903
3. eight
4. gray
5. $1,000, utilities provided
6. Hawk's Nest Drive

Dining Out
1. d, c, b, a
2. Vonda Dudley Wix
3. True

Crimes and Victims
1. He is "pushed off his own mountain."
2. Hugh Lumpton/Qwill believes Hugh killed Hawkinfield to protect himself and his father.
3. Sherry Hawkinfield, the victim's daughter.
4. Qwills grabs the iron candelabrum and pokes it "into his attacker's midriff . . ." and then hits him with a burl bowl.

THE CAT WHO WASN'T THERE
General Questions
1. 16.
2. "He was of medium build, and . . . [had] a bearded face."
3. Massachusetts.
4. According to superstition, "it brings bad luck to the company that stages it."
5. "That she shot a man twenty-odd years ago and was charged with murder, but the Hasselriches bribed the judge to let her off without a sentence."
6. "It was registered to one Charles Edward Martin of Charlestown, Massachusetts."
7. First, she sees "a journey across water . . . with stormy weather ahead . . . [and] some kind of fraud . . . or treachery."
8. Grace Utley.
9. Eleven.
10. Day six.
11. Melinda Goodwinter.
12. "Between nine-thirty and ten," Koko let out "an unearthly howl . . . in the shower." Qwill realizes that Koko had howled at the exact moment Irma died in Scotland.
13. Bruce, the bus driver.
14. Polly finds a letter in Irma's briefcase that is from Bruce's sister, Katie. She shows this letter to Qwill.

15. "Well, one of them stole my emery boards—a whole pack of them, one at a time."

16. The card with the woman in a grape arbor, the nine of pentacles or, as Qwill remarks, "The nine of diamonds! The Curse of Scotland."

17. He learns her full name, Katie Gow MacBean, from Polly, who has gotten Irma's address book from her parents.

18. She shredded it.

19. Melinda Goodwinter/She was buried in the Hasselrich "family plot with full obsequies."

20. Nick Bamba.

21. That she might be smuggling drugs.

22. Hornbuckle tells Qwill that "After the boy died, the doctor kep' sendin' me to the bank, reg'lar, once a month."

23. Ronald Frobnitz.

24. "The chewed remains of Tiny Tim . . . his favorite toy."

25. There was a "pervading stink . . . [that] had a distinct overtone of cat—nervous cat!"

26. While at the Goodwinter sale, "Qwill realized that the beard disguised a long, narrow face, known in Moose County as the Goodwinter face."

27. That it had "been removed from the filing cabinet."

28. Her references to "the smell of blood and a damned spot she could never wash out" were lines from the play that suggested her guilt, according to Qwill.

29. Koko shredded it.

Chronological Order of Events
3, 1, 6, 2, 7, 8, 13, 11, 10, 9, 14, 4, 5, 12, 15, 16, 21, 18, 19, 20, 17, 23, 22, 24

Koko and Yum Yum
1. He stares "pointedly at his empty plate. . . . Qwilleran gave them a handful of crunchy cereal concocted by . . . Mildred. . . . As he watched them munching and waving their tails in rapture, an idea struck him."
2. Koko.
3. The cats licked it clean. An example of their so-called "wet-cleaning."
4. She thinks the cats "probably slept on top of the dryer until they were half-cooked."
5. When playing the tape that describes how Dr. Cream was noted for using pink pills, "Koko interrupted with a stern 'Yow-w-w.' "

Women in Qwill's Life
P, M, M, M, M, P, P, P

Dining Out
b, f, c, d, a, e

Crimes and Victims

1. Murder.
2. Melinda Goodwinter.
3. His theory is "that she tampered with some vitamin capsules that Polly had taken to Scotland, substituting a drug that would stop the heart."
4. Qwill believes, "It was guilt that drove her over the edge."
5. Yes, "but not the murder."
6. True.

THE CAT WHO WENT INTO THE CLOSET
General Questions

1. James Qwilleran.
2. Hixie Rice.
3. Hixie Rice.
4. He got the information from "some files that belonged to Euphonia Gage's father-in-law . . . he neglected to say that Koko pried his way into a certain closet."
5. Purple.
6. Mildred Hanstable.
7. On Christmas Eve.
8. Qwill reminds Arch that Polly and he "prefer singlehood."
9. Park of Pink Sunsets.
10. Wetherby Goode.
11. She "had developed a passion for the greyhound races!"
12. Celia Robinson.
13. Inchpot/Gil Inchpot.
14. At the airport "in the parking structure."
15. Claude owns it./Betty manages it.
16. Mr. Crocus.
17. She left them "a hundred dollars apiece."
18. She leaves everything to "The Park of Pink Sunsets . . . to build, equip, and maintain a health spa for the residents."
19. He "followed the tracks" to a hollow, "and what he found there sent him running back to the car." Qwill discovered Gil Inchpot's body.
20. They were "gatecrashers at the preview" of the show.
21. "Thirty-two inches of snow fell in sixteen hours."
22. "A jeweler's box containing a man's gold ring . . . a signet, with an intricate design on the crown."
23. Qwilleran.
24. 3, 1, 2, 4
25. "Many of Koko's discoveries were associated with feet."
26. According to Rhoda Tibbett, Lena "died of cancer a few years ago."
27. November 27/Nancy knows "because it was . . . [her] mother's birthday."

28. That her mother, Lena, was in actuality Lethe, and was Mrs. Gage's daughter, making Nancy Euphonia Gage's granddaughter.
29. He called Celia Robinson and told her that he would be gone for the weekend. "Her phone really was tapped, and they'd [the robbers] connect my name with the Gage mansion."
30. Clayton's taped conversation with Mr. Crocus provided information about the blackmail and that a family secret caused it. Crocus also said that she told Claude, and he said he could stop it.
31. George Brezes.

Chronological Order of Events

1, 8, 3, 5, 17, 9, 11, 2, 6, 7, 10, 12, 13, 14, 15, 16, 4

Koko and Yum Yum

1. Koko
2. Koko
3. Koko
4. Oh Jay
5. Wrigley

Women in Qwill's Life

1. "In the carriage house at the rear of the Gage property."
2. Polly.
3. Vice President of Advertising and Promotion.
4. She was preparing to elope.
5. A lavaliere and earrings: "fiery black opals rimmed with discreet diamonds."

Qwill's Living Quarters

1. An abundance of closets
2. Junior Goodwinter
3. Fifty
4. d, a, b, c

Dining Out

1. c, d, d, a, a, a, b, b, b
2. It was "a recipe for . . . angel food cake with chocolate frosting."

Crimes and Victims

1. No.
2. "Rob 'em and rub 'em out!"
3. "It could have been a drop of poison in her Dubonnet. She always had to have her aperitif before dinner."
4. Pete, the assistant at the Park of the Pink Sunsets.
5. Claude, who was present with Betty the weekend Inchpot disappeared.
6. There "was a gunshot to the head."

CHARACTER IDENTIFICATION III

1. Chase W. Amberton
2. Mrs. Ascott
3. Hilary VanBrook
4. Zella Chisholm and Grace Chisholm Utley
5. Jessica Tuttle
6. Celia Robinson
7. Clayton
8. Jack and Pug Goodwinter
9. Nancy Fincher Inchpot
10. Scott Gippel
11. Mildred Hanstable
12. Jerome Todd
13. Homer Tibbitt
14. Fiona Stucker
15. Adelaide St. John Plumb
16. Hugh Lumpton
17. Karl Oscar Klaus
18. Randy Jupiter
19. Dennis Hough
20. Sherry Hawkinfield
21. Bruce Gow
22. Mr. and Mrs. Glinko
23. Vonda Dudley Wix
24. Bruce Scott
25. Irma Hasselrich

CLUES, CLUES, CLUES III

1. *The Cat Who Knew a Cardinal*
2. *The Cat Who Went Into the Closet*
3. *The Cat Who Wasn't There*
4. *The Cat Who Moved a Mountain*
5. *The Cat Who Lived High*

PLACES, PLACES, PLACES III

1. Amy's Lunch Bucket
2. Bid-a-Bit Auctions
3. Spudsboro
4. Sawdust City
5. Shantytown
6. Potato Cove
7. Purple Point
8. Hawk's Nest Drive
9. In Potato Cove
10. Tacky Tack Shop
11. Park of Pink Sunsets
12. Klingenschoen Professional Building
13. Indian Village
14. East Shore Condominiums
15. Penniman Plaza

QWILL QUIZ III

1. Qwill's car that is stolen, crashed, and burned.
2. One night he was drunk and fell off a subway platform. Passengers waiting for the train pulled him out of the way of an oncoming train.
3. Red ones.
4. d, c, c, b, a
5. He wants to "get away from it all for a while" and to contemplate his purpose in life and his future.
6. He thinks it might provide him with an interesting angle for a column.
7. Qwill sold ties at Macy's and baseball programs at Comiskey Park.
8. No, but when Moose County residents hear inaccurately that Qwill died in an accident, he realizes that "his extended family included the entire population of Moose County."

9. True.
10. False.
11. Castles.
12. True.

THE FACTS ABOUT POLLY DUNCAN
1. She is the head librarian.
2. 25 years.
3. Orville.
4. Hippolyta.
5. Two: Desdemona and Ophelia.
6. Alice Blue.
7. Catta and Bootsie/Brutus.
8. Sonnets.
9. True.
10. She had bronchitis and asthma.
11. A cup of tea and a Lorna Doone.
12. Sarah.

THE FACTS ABOUT THE RIKERS
1. On Christmas Eve.
2. He is the feature editor.
3. Rosie.
4. Amanda Goodwinter.
5. Publisher.
6. Charles Schulz.
7. Mildred taught home economics and fine arts at Pickax High School.
8. For almost 30 years.
9. She drops pennies here and there.
10. Sunny Daze.
11. To knit socks.
12. A collection of tin objects/collectibles.

THE FACTS ABOUT FRAN (FRANCESCA) BRODIE
1. She is an assistant at Amanda's Studio of Interior Design.
2. Chief Brodie.
3. Anne Boleyn.
4. Strawberry blond.
5. The Pickax Theatre Club.
6. The lead.
7. Chicago.
8. True.
9. True.
10. True.

THE CAT WHO CAME TO BREAKFAST
General Questions
1. 66.
2. True.
3. In Oregon with her old college roommate.
4. Fifteen guests become ill from food poisoning, and a man drowns in the hotel pool.
5. A front step caved in, and a guest fell and broke a rib. Nick wants Qwill to "go to the island and snoop around."

6. Thoreau's *Walden* and Anatole France's *Penguin Island*.
7. A cabin cruiser blew up in the marina, and its owner was killed.
8. Domino Inn.
9. Four Pips.
10. Buccaneer Den.
11. Corsair Room and Smugglers' Cove.
12. Dwight Somers.
13. Qwill buys two Venetian masks and a glass tray.
14. According to Qwill, "Any individual in the business world who declined free publicity in his column was suspect."
15. June Halliburton.
16. Yum Yum found a rusty nail in a crevice, worked it out, and then pushed it into another crevice.
17. Before Commercialization.
18. The Applehardts.
19. Providence Island; it was so named by the first settlers when "A divine providence cast 'em up on the beach after their ship was wrecked."
20. In Providence Village.
21. Breakfast Island/Pear Island/Providence Island/Grand Island Club.
22. 66.
23. Derek Cuttlebrink.
24. He places a sock on the floor, crumples Qwill's trousers and puts them on the floor next to the bedside table, and then wads his shirt up and puts it under the dresser.
25. He finds "a silver pen and a leatherbound book stamped in gold: 'E. C. Applehardt.'"
26. At the lighthouse.
27. An adult male was shot while "hang gliding on the sand dune at the north end of the island."
28. "Gumbo."
29. There is a local phone number written on the paper. Based on the handwriting and the fact that the paper looked "like a piece of music manuscript," Qwill believes the note belongs to June Halliburton.
30. Cage: Elizabeth's middle name.
31. "One looks like my brother William, and one looks like Jack."
32. Miss Double-Six.
33. "The only people who got sick were the ones that ordered chicken gumbo. The shrimp gumbo—no trouble!"
34. Only the hazelnuts.
35. "He decided that the lightkeepers had wandered into the bog themselves."
36. George duLac.
37. Filed/hack and blade.
38. Her maiden name is Kale. She is originally from Providence Island. Her father is the caretaker at The Pines.

39. June and Noisette.
40. Filed, hack, blade, cage, Elijah, Jack, and kale.

Chronological Order of Events
1, 8, 2, 6, 7, 5, 3, 4, 9, 10, 11, 15, 12, 13, 14

Koko and Yum Yum
1. Koko
2. Koko/Yum Yum
3. Yum Yum

Women in Qwill's Life
1. Her college roommate. Her name is Sarah, and she is a residential architect.
2. Only one short one.
3. She directs the music programs.
4. She directs the music and entertaining at Pear Island Resort.
5. She has decided to build a house. Sarah designed the house while Polly was in Oregon.

Qwill's Living Quarters
1. There are seven rooms, two suites, and five cottages.
2. The door is painted black with white pips (dots), like on a domino.
3. True.
4. True.

Dining Out
a, b, b, b, a, a, c

Crimes and Victims
1. Fifteen.
2. George duLac.
3. Reverend Harding.
4. Qwill believes "the crimes are being committed by a coalition" intent on stopping the resort development.
5. Jack Applehardt.
6. Elijah Kale.
7. She refuses to divorce him.
8. Elijah Kale.

THE CAT WHO BLEW THE WHISTLE
General Questions
1. XYZ Enterprises.
2. He opened Lumbertown Credit Union.
3. 3, 4, 2, 1

4. e, a, b, c, d
5. He might write a book about "train wrecks . . . [and] the nostalgia of the Steam Era when trains were the glamorous mode of transportation."
6. Floyd Trevelyan.
7. In Indian Village.
8. Amanda and Fran/Amanda's Studio of Interior Design.
9. Nella Hooper/Texas.
10. Yes.
11. When he finds Koko sitting on the story about the Lumbertown Credit Union and the photo of Trevelyan in the *Moose County Something*. He circled the newspaper three times, doing what Qwill calls his "death dance."
12. Benno.
13. Zak.
14. He tells him he is a writer.
15. He asks if she might be interested in working as a companion to elderly shut-ins.
16. A twistletwig rocker.
17. Operation Whistle.
18. Decoys Polly brought to Qwill from Oregon.
19. The lights went out.
20. He tells Ozzie that he is preparing to write a book on railroading in the Age of Steam.
21. Sawdust City and Lockmaster railroad line.
22. True.
23. A column on sunburn.
24. He wants her to ask if Nella Hooper's apartment is vacant or if it will be vacant soon and when Eddie Trevelyan moved in.
25. The Lumbertown Credit Union.
26. Qwill.
27. Clues include Koko's vigil at the window, Koko's digging in the crook of Qwill's elbow, Koko's interest in the Panama Canal, and Koko's running to the concrete slab of the driveway.
28. Hermia.

Chronological Order of Events
1, 2, 3, 4, 5, 15, 8, 9, 11, 12, 13, 6, 7, 14, 16, 10, 17

Koko and Yum Yum
1. Yum Yum.
2. There is a power outage in the whole county.
3. They "fall into line behind him, marching with tails at twelve o'clock."
4. Usually one-third.
5. Koko/Yum Yum.

Women in Qwill's Life
1. Celia Robinson
2. Polly
3. Worrying/exercising
4. She has a mild heart attack.
5. Dr. Diane Lanspeak
6. At the Duncan home with her sister-in-law, Lynette Duncan

Qwill's Living Quarters
1. True
2. True
3. True
4. True

Dining Out
1. Kabibbles
2. It was started ten years earlier by women who weren't allowed to play pool at the Trackside Tavern.
3. a, a, b, b, b, a, a, a

Crimes and Victims
1. He is knifed at Trackside Tavern.
2. True.
3. Benno.
4. Apparently he was attacked by a horned owl.
5. He believes "forensic experts will say he was killed by a blow, or blows, to the head, inflicted by a carpenter's hammer."
6. Benno/James Henry Ducker.
7. Eddie Trevelyan.
8. Benno.
9. Apparently because Benno didn't get the money he was promised for killing Floyd, he attacked Eddie, and when Eddie tried to get away, he accidentally killed Benno.
10. Lionella Hooper or Lionel Hooper.

THE CAT WHO SAID CHEESE
General Questions
1. Black.
2. The sinking of the *Titanic*, war in Europe, and the assassination of President Kennedy.
3. Gustav Limburger.
4. Polly.
5. He buries it because it smells like Limburger cheese. Even the cats wrinkled their noses at the smell of it.
6. Qwill tells him that he'd "like to write a history of the famous hotel."
7. Gingerbread Alley.
8. Elaine Fetter.

9. Restaurant Management.
10. Wild honeybees.
11. Aubrey Scotten.
12. Nick Bamba.
13. The Spoonery.
14. At his cabin.
15. She is reading a cookbook. She tells Qwill to call her Onoosh.
16. She spent her honeymoon there.
17. Room 203.
18. Anne Marie Toms, Lenny Inchpot's girlfriend.
19. The mystery lady.
20. Ona Dolman.
21. Lenny Inchpot and the florist who sold the suspect the flowers.
22. "It happened while he was in the Navy. He had an accident, and his hair turned white overnight." He "got clunked on the head and dumped in the ocean and nearly drowned."
23. Sarah, the office manager.
24. All statements are correct.
25. Koko has 30./Yum Yum has 24.
26. The Pasty Parlor/There was a protest against "subversive ingredients in the filling."
27. Franklin Pickett.
28. When Qwill checks his three pledge cards for the bike-a-thon, he finds only two. The third one, Lenny's, is "on the floor—well chewed."
29. There are two categories: with and without turnips. Mildred disqualifies an entry because it contains turkey. "Dark meat of turkey!" Traditionally a pasty "calls for beef or pork."
30. $1,500/Sarah, the office manager, bids for and wins the date with Qwill.
31. He died from bee stings. His body was found at a rental cabin owned by the Scottens on the bank of Black Creek.
32. Victor Greer.
33. Elaine Fetter.
34. The missing notebook of recipes belonging to Iris Cobb.
35. Celia Robinson.
36. Sarah tells Qwill that she was a preliminary judge in the pasty contest, and there was one pasty that "tasted as good as Iris Cobb's!" This causes Qwill to inquire about who cooked this pasty. He learns that Elaine Fetter cooked it.
37. $10,000.
38. Donald, Elaine Fetter's son.
39. Vic was the man who saved Aubrey from drowning.
40. In the frozen turkey delivered to Qwill's house.
41. Lenny Inchpot.
42. Her real name was Ona Dolmathakia. She was Vic Greer's former wife.
43. To his daughter in Germany.

Chronological Order of Events
Answers: 12, 9, 6, 3, 4, 1, 7, 2, 5, 8, 10, 13, 16, 19, 15, 14, 11, 17, 18, 20

Koko and Yum Yum
1. Yum Yum.
2. No.
3. The faster he jumps, the more urgent the call.
4. *Stalking the Wild Asparagus* and *A Taste of Honey*.
5. Gruyere, Brie, and feta.

Women in Qwill's Life
1. Qwill replies that their cats are incompatible and they are happy being single.
2. "Book withdrawals are privileged information."
3. Boss-lady.
4. In a condominium at Indian Village.
5. Public-access computers.

Qwill's Living Quarters
1. A cupola
2. Qwill's private suite

Dining Out
1. Lori Bamba's The Spoonery.
2. Amusing trout, serious steak, spinach in phyllo pastry, brussels sprouts with caraway, turnip souffle, sesame seed salad, poached pears.
3. She brought her "some gourmet mushroom soup!"
4. The Old Stone Mill.

Crimes and Victims
1. Vic Greer.
2. Onoosh Dolmathakia.
3. Vic Greer.
4. Aubrey Scotten.
5. He got drunk, and Aubrey carried him to the cabin. Aubrey put a wool blanket on him, which antagonized the bees, and he was stung to death.
6. He says to Koko, "Okay, we'll play a game. If Aubrey purposely caused Victor Greer's death, blink!" In the end, "Koko won. Aubrey was absolved."

THE CAT WHO TAILED A THIEF
General Questions
1. He suspects "punks from Chipmunk" or a "gang from Lockmaster" or "kids that hang around George Breze's dump."
2. A Russian novel titled *A Thief*.
3. A medium-sized van.

4. "Carpenter Gothic."
5. $2,000.
6. He puts on his "right shoe before the left."
7. She gave him a set of leather-bound books by Herman Melville, printed in 1924, and an opera recording of *Adriana Lecourvreur* with Renata Tebaldi.
8. A sporran.
9. Sara Plensdorf, the office manager at the *Moose County Something*.
10. Gil MacMurchie.
11. The dirk with the silver lion.
12. Danielle Carmichael.
13. Polly, Lynette, Qwill, Mildred Riker, Amanda.
14. Hixie Rice.
15. The Nouvelle Dining Club.
16. Walking down a street in Detroit.
17. There was an "anonymous tip on the hotline" suggesting that "the manager's locker at Indian Village clubhouse" be searched. The items reported stolen were in the locker.
18. *Short & Tall Tales*.
19. Danielle.
20. Ernie Kemple.
21. "In Lenny Inchpot's possession," in his locker at Indian Village.
22. $20,000 plus the amount charged by the contractor to do the work.
23. In New Orleans.
24. This is a danger signal, and he is trying to tell you something.
25. George Breze.
26. Four ways.
27. Joe Bunker.
28. One of the cats throws up a hairball on the photos. To Qwill, this was "a new low! A breach of etiquette!"
29. Celia Robinson.
30. When Carter Lee is wining and dining Tracy Kemple, she gives him the doll as a good-luck token.
31. Danielle.
32. The silver-hilted dirk she stole from the MacMurchie house.
33. Danielle/After listening to Clayton's tape recording, it is obvious to Qwill that Danielle is the kleptomaniac.
34. Sarah Plensdorf.
35. The investigators found that he was not connected "whatever with the preservation/restoration field."
36. From the Cavendish sisters.
37. The historic Pickax Hotel and the Limburger Mansion.
38. "Go, and get in the car!"
39. Qwill yells there is a witness upstairs, and as Carter Lee turns to look, Koko swoops down on his head and howls and scratches him.

40. Their Land Rover is "trapped between the crotch of the ancient tree and an enormous boulder" at the bridge they attempt to cross.

Chronological Order of Events
10, 1, 5, 6, 7, 2, 3, 16, 8, 9, 4, 11, 14, 13, 15, 12, 17, 18, 19

Koko and Yum Yum
1. Yum Yum
2. Koko
3. Mosca
4. Yum Yum
5. Yum Yum
6. Koko

Women in Qwill's Life
1. A suede suit with a silk blouse
2. A 1924 set of leather-bound books by Melville and an opera recording of *Adriana Lecourvreur*
3. Brutus
4. Catta

Qwill's Living Quarters
1. It is too difficult to heat evenly.
2. Indian Village.
3. Unit Four, Building Five.
4. Fran Brodie.
5. To a honey color.
6. The dining alcove.

Dining Out
1. c, a, b, d, e, f
2. Seventeen
3. Onoosh's Mediterranean Café
4. The Northern Lights Hotel

Crimes and Victims
1. Willard Carmichael/He is held up and shot in Detroit.
2. A hit man supposedly hired by Carter Lee James.
3. Koko was frequently hitting Yum Yum.
4. Carter Lee poisons Lynette.
5. Murder and fraud.
6. She turns state's witness, although she is the real petty thief.
7. *The Thief*, *The Confidence Man*, and *Ossian and the Ossianic Literature*.

THE CAT WHO SANG FOR THE BIRDS
General Questions
1. A 1939 copy of Nathaniel West's *The Day of the Locust*.
2. *The Crucible*.
3. Over ninety.

4. The K Foundation bought the house and "gave it to the local art community as a center."
5. Beverly Forfar.
6. Jasper.
7. The artist who is commissioned to paint Polly's portrait.
8. Hixie Rice.
9. *The Pacific War, Fire Over London, The Last 100 Days.*
10. Jasper Westrup.
11. Phoebe Sloan.
12. Winslow Homer.
13. Ronald Frobnitz.
14. That he "wanted an outing."
15. "A dark red splotch."
16. Small figure drawings were missing; "there had been a dozen or more."
17. Thornton Haggis.
18. *Fire Over London.*
19. The Coggin farmhouse burned down.
20. The photo showing Mrs. Coggin digging a hole, with a coffee can beside her.
21. "Five bundles of bills totaling a hundred thousand dollars."
22. Northern Land Improvement/The agreement was that the land would remain for agricultural use only.
23. Koko is sitting on a book titled *Mark Twain A to Z.* On the cover of the book is Twain with his great moustache.
24. Shafthouses.
25. Jasper Westrup and Derek Cuttlebrink.
26. "He suddenly nipped the thumb holding the book."
27. Endangered species of butterflies.
28. *Baseball, An Illustrated History*/Koko had been keeping the book warm, then jumped down and ran around in circles.
29. This is the name Jake uses to refer to Phoebe.
30. Margaret Ramsbottom.
31. She was "wearing long sleeves all of a sudden" and wasn't herself.
32. $6,000 an acre.
33. The north star points west.
34. Mrs. Fish-eye, Qwill's tenth-grade teacher.
35. The new fire chief in Pickax. He is his brother-in-law.
36. A recumbent bicycle.
37. From the information Phoebe sent him in her letter.
38. The *Whiteness of White* intaglio won by Frobnitz in the Art Center raffle.
39. Katie and Mac.

Chronological Order of Events

3, 1, 8, 14, 20, 21, 12, 2, 5, 6, 4, 7, 9, 11, 10, 18, 19, 15, 13, 16, 17, 22, 23

Koko and Yum Yum

1. He carries them in a white canvas tote bag.
2. Yum Yum.
3. Kek-kek-kek-kek.
4. Sixteen seconds.
5. Four.

Women in Qwill's Life

1. A handkerchief that belonged to his grandmother
2. Blue silk
3. *Hamlet*
4. On the weekends

Qwill's Living Quarters

1. The "Guggenheim of Moose County"
2. Eight
3. Kevin Doone

Dining Out

1. He found two small yellow cartons in the trash container.
2. Chet's Bar and Barbecue.
3. b, a, c, c, b, c, a, a

Crimes and Victims

1. *Fire Over London.*
2. A blow to the head.
3. The needle of the compass pointing to the west and the two books whose authors were Rebecca West and Nathaniel West.
4. Jake Westrup.
5. One count of arson and two counts of homicide.
6. Qwill grabs a totem pole and hits the intruder. Koko jumps on his back and digs his claws in.
7. Koko began to bleat like "a dirty old ram."
8. Chief Brodie "says that Chester Ramsbottom will be implicated in the Coggin incident."

CHARACTER IDENTIFICATION IV

1. Floyd Trevelyan
2. Virginia Alstock
3. Lenore Bassett
4. Roger MacGillivray
5. Gil McMurchie
6. Whannell MacWhannell
7. Mr. Pat O'Dell
8. Jack Nibble
9. Jerry Sip
10. Homer Tibbitt
11. Carter Lee James
12. Lionella "Nella" Hooper
13. James Henry Ducker
14. Ruth and Jenny Cavendish
15. Sarah Plensdorf

CLUES, CLUES, CLUES IV

1. *The Cat Who Sang for the Birds*
2. *The Cat Who Blew the Whistle*
3. *The Cat Who Came to Breakfast*
4. *The Cat Who Said Cheese*
5. *The Cat Who Tailed a Thief*

PLACES, PLACES, PLACES IV

1. Antiques by Noisette
2. Chet's Bar and Barbecue
3. Stables Row
4. The Spoonery
5. Trackside Tavern
6. Scottie's Men's Store
7. Sip 'n' Nibble
8. Pickax Peoples' Bank
9. Pickax Public Library
10. Pear Island Resort
11. Onoosh's Mediterranean Café
12. Palomino Paddock
13. Northern Land Improvement
14. Nouvelle Dining Club
15. Moose County Community College
16. Limburger Mansion
17. Great Food Explo
18. Click Club
19. Northern Lights Hotel

QWILL QUIZ IV

1. A "cat opera for TV."
2. In Moose County.
3. Marconi.
4. Feet/left/right.
5. Late/late.
6. *Short & Tall Tales*.
7. A jazz pianist.
8. Mrs. Fish-eye and Aunt Fannie Klingenschoen.
9. True.
10. False. He reminds Junior when he inquires about Qwill's plan to get a word processor that he likes his electric typewriter.
11. Steam Age of Railroading/Moose County Legends/Pickax Hotel.
12. All are correct.

THE FACTS ABOUT HIXIE RICE

1. French
2. Advertising Manager
3. Vice President of Advertising and Promotion
4. True
5. 3, 4, 2, 1, 5

THE FACTS ABOUT DEREK CUTTLEBRINK

1. Six foot seven, six foot four, six foot eight.
2. Moose County Community College/Restaurant Management.
3. Check all except for teacher, stockbroker, and musician.

4. Five.
5. The visitor.
6. Qwill.
7. He is the assistant manager.
8. Elizabeth Cage.
9. Hams.
10. He is the maître d'.

CATS, CATS, CATS
1. Polly
2. Polly
3. Maggie Sprenkle
4. Maggie Sprenkle
5. Pickax Library cats
6. Wetherby Goode
7. Maggie Sprenkle
8. Emma Huggins Wimsey
9. The Bambas at Nutcracker Inn
10. Maggie Sprenkle
11. Mildred and Arch Riker
12. Eddington Smith/the Bethunes

THE CAT WHO SAW STARS
General Questions
1. Fishport.
2. Jill Handley.
3. David.
4. True.
5. Benjamin Franklin.
6. *A Connecticut Yankee in King Arthur's Court, A Horse's Tale,* and *Jumping Frog.*
7. *A Visit to a Small Planet.*
8. Ontario, Canada/her sister.
9. Top o' the Dunes Club.
10. Sunny Daze.
11. Socks.
12. The Snuggery.
13. Sandpit Road.
14. Floats in the July Fourth parade.
15. Koko.
16. David/21/Philadelphia.
17. Four days/"There was no decomposition."
18. He worked with computers, but his hobby was UFOs.
19. Skewered potatoes.
20. Mark Twain.
21. An embroidered copy of words from one of his semiannual columns on cats.
22. It was so negative, Elizabeth didn't give her an honest interpretation.
23. Mona/Desdemona.
24. The *Viewfinder.*
25. The *Suncatcher.*

26. He suggests it is the result of a mechanical blast of air from the visitors.
27. Qwill understood the connection immediately after Unc Huggins referred to Bowen as a "horse's tail."
28. She wants to produce an animated film about crows.
29. Tubby.
30. He finds a "crack in the top surface of the mantel."
31. *Oedipus Rex, Macbeth, Major Barbara*, and *The Importance of Being Earnest*.
32. The ones with portraits of the two Irish playwrights.
33. Mayor.
34. Einstein.
35. He sits down, an indication that there is something there.
36. He knocks it off the wall.
37. Just "the grocer boy."
38. Her dad's collection of "everything that was ever printed about UFOs."
39. Barb Ogilvie and Ernestine Bowen.
40. *Far From the Madding Crowd*.
41. Qwill.
42. Pirate Shoals.
43. A vest in the Mackintosh clan tartan.

Chronological Order of Events
18, 17, 16, 15, 8, 10, 9, 13, 14, 11, 12, 7, 6, 1, 2, 3, 4, 5

Koko and Yum Yum
1. Koko
2. Yum Yum
3. Because there is sand from the beach
4. Yum Yum
5. A stuffed calico kitten toy
6. Yum Yum with Gertrude

Women in Qwill's Life
1. He complained that on previous trips he seldom heard from her.
2. Dr. Teresa Bunker.
3. Teresa begins to cook for him.
4. About the professor in Canada that convinced her to stay longer in Quebec City.
5. Tea/coffee.

Qwill's Living Quarters
1. True.
2. True.
3. Three.
4. A frame of two-by-fours with loose sand for steps.
5. Qwill doesn't want to encourage visitors.
6. The Snuggery.

Dining Out
f, d, d, d, a, b, e, c

Crimes and Victims
1. No.
2. She is killed when her RV falls into the sinkhole and she is buried in the sand.
3. That he was involved with a Florida drug ring.

THE CAT WHO ROBBED A BANK
General Questions
1. Pickax's first-ever Mark Twain Festival and the tri-county Scottish Gathering and Highland Games.
2. A calendar.
3. True.
4. True.
5. *Night Must Fall.*
6. There is an animal in each saying.
7. Mark Twain Suite.
8. Mackintosh Inn.
9. Gustav Stickley.
10. Paul Skumble.
11. Barry Morghan.
12. Daisy.
13. Five.
14. Bernhardt, Brontë, Nation, MacDonald, Alcott.
15. Covered dish.
16. He thinks he should "go as a security guard."
17. He buys "a foot-tall container of classical shape" called a vessel.
18. M. R.
19. His niece.
20. Polly, Dr. Diane, Susan Exbridge, and Maggie Sprenkle.
21. L'Heure Bleue.
22. A cameo ring.
23. "Boze, short for Bozo."
24. Ms. North.
25. While reading from the play *Night Must Fall.* When Qwill reads the lines, "Suddenly he picked up a cushion and smothered his rich employer," Koko's "YOW!" caused Qwill to remark, "he knew—more about the murder than the investigators had revealed."
26. She "saw streaks of light behind the blinds in two of the windows on the third floor—like beams of a flashlight moving around."
27. Her "clothes and things are still in the room, and the rental car's still here on the lot . . . [and] the jewel cases are still in the manager's safe."

28. d, e, a, b, c
29. The round covered bowl of spalted maple that Qwill wanted to buy at the craft fair.
30. Mildred.
31. Two of Carol's French perfume bottles.
32. A book dealer from Boston.
33. He puts fang marks on them and then scatters them about the floor.
34. In the spalted maple box.
35. "All the towels were gone from both bathrooms—bath towels, face towels, everything."
36. To Rio/He is taking an airplane.
37. The collection belonged to Maggie Sprenkle.
38. Kiltie, the Scotsman bank.
39. An old-fashioned file box labeled "Klingenschoen Correspondence."
40. Her revolver.
41. Boze.
42. Dana.
43. Polly, Arch, and Mildred, respectively.
44. Donald/Nora.
45. He killed his father./Delacamp.
46. *Oedipus Rex*.
47. A foil gum-wrapper.
48. Lenny finds a foil gum wrapper.
49. He was shot and fell in front of a bus when attempting to rob a bank.
50. Harriet Marie Penney.

Chronological Order of Events
1, 4, 20, 9, 15, 2, 3, 8, 11, 16, 17, 18, 19, 12, 5, 10, 6, 13, 7, 14

Koko and Yum Yum
1. Koko.
2. Yum Yum.
3. Yum Yum.
4. Koko.
5. So Yum Yum can't tip it over when searching for hidden treasures.
6. Yum Yum "prowls aimlessly," and Koko slaps his tail against the floor impatiently.

Women in Qwill's Life
1. A pair of paisley silk pajamas with a "mushy" card from Koko and Yum Yum.
2. Polly wears a shoulder sash in the Robertson tartan. Because she is a Duncan by marriage, and the leader of the Robertson clan was Duncan of Atholia, Polly wears this tartan.

3. Qwill gave Polly opals from Delacamp's firm.
4. He ordered a spray bottle of L'Heure Bleue.

Qwill's Living Quarters
1. The windows are in the shapes of triangles and rhomboids.
2. On the back of the building.

Dining Out
1. At Onoosh's restaurant.
2. Macaroni and cheese and meat loaf.
3. Carol Lanspeak.
4. Meat-filled pastry turnovers, like pasties, but without the potatoes.
5. It is "five small courses and an adventure in tasting."
6. Celia.
7. Mildred/Arch and Mildred invite Qwill and Polly to dinner to meet Kirt Nightingale.
8. Rennie's.

Crimes and Victims
1. Boze.
2. b, a, c, a, d, a
3. One scenario has him falling to his death in the mine. Another scenario might be that he commited suicide. Each is plausible; neither is certain from the text.

THE CAT WHO SMELLED A RAT
General Questions
1. The Big One.
2. A carved wooden box with the words *Love Box* (the *g* is hidden on it).
3. They vandalized the XYZ billboard at the city limits. They "went out after dark and pasted a twelve-foot patch over it, saying, 'We stand under our roofs with a bucket.'"
4. Hixie Rice.
5. 10/1850.
6. *Mysteries of the Egyptian Pyramids.*
7. They are each direct descendants of a mine owner.
8. "Q-Tips."
9. Misty Morghan/Barry Morghan.
10. Maggie Sprenkle.
11. A Danish rug and the porcelain parrots for Polly.
12. He "was hoping [Maggie would] . . . donate the French crystal pitcher."
13. He dies of a heart attack.
14. Theo Morghan, brother of Barry Morghan, and David Todd.
15. Donex & Associates.

16. Ronald Frobnitz.
17. Kirt Nightingale.
18. Koko knocks one of the potted geraniums off of the balcony railing.
19. First, Koko knocks another geranium off the balcony, and then while Qwill cleans up the broken potted geranium, Koko shreds the editorial in the newspaper.
20. He topples a table lamp, bunches the Danish rug, and scatters red pillows, wooden apples, magazines, and desktop papers on the floor. There were also geraniums in the kitchen sink.
21. Eddington Smith's cat.
22. Two: *Two Robins with Worm* and *Two Robins without Worm*.
23. She thought it was "repulsive."
24. Henry Zoller.
25. She tells Qwill that "he's had cosmetic surgery. . . . I can tell his whole face has been reconstructed."
26. Ralph Abbey.
27. He wanted to convert the property into an antique village.
28. Cass's mother, an accountant and astrologer.
29. Cass Young.
30. She says that Zoller and Young "disagreed with Don a lot. . . . They had a violent argument over the payday loan company. . . . Don said it was legal . . . Dr. Zoller said it was unethical and immoral . . . he and Cass resigned."
31. The wooden glove box.
32. When Koko sits in the box, his body seems "elevated as if on a cushion."/Qwill discovers a false bottom in the box.
33. "One of the cats was 'sleighriding,' or 'bottomsliding,' as it was sometimes called."
34. An envelope addressed to Helen Omblower.
35. They tell Qwill that a "recreation center"—"a video palace with gambling machines"—is planned, and it will be called "The Shafthouse."
36. Homer Tibbitt.
37. Gideon Blake, alias Gregory Blythe; George Omblower, alias Kirt Nightingale; and Don Exbridge.
38. Qwill tells Nightingale he is planning to establish a rare book room at the library in memory of Eddington Smith.
39. The martini pitcher.
40. Gregory Blythe.

Chronological Order of Events
8, 9, 1, 2, 3, 6, 13, 16, 17, 4, 5, 11, 14, 10, 12, 18, 19, 7, 15, 20

Koko and Yum Yum
1. Koko.
2. Koko.
3. Yum Yum.
4. Koko.
5. They do not want to travel.
6. Yum Yum.
7. Lengthwise.

Women in Qwill's Life
1. He shops for her, and she invites him to dinner.
2. Select from the following: He can't divulge who writes Derek's songs/he doesn't discuss Koko's "remarkable intuition"/he doesn't tell Polly that he is Ronald Frobnitz/he doesn't always tell her about his unofficial investigations/and he doesn't tell Polly how his hunches often begin as twitches in his moustache.
3. Qwill.
4. From her in-laws.

Qwill's Living Quarters
1. Unit Four in the Willows unit.
2. Polly lives in Unit One/Kirt Nightingale lives in Unit Two/Wetherby Goode lives in Unit Three.
3. Fran Brodie.
4. It's "in Siamese colors."

Dining Out
1. Tipsy's Tavern.
2. In Brrr township.
3. It was the Limburger Mansion.
4. e, d, c, b, a
5. Mrs. Stebbins.

Crimes and Victims
1. "Perhaps twenty-five years. Time flies."
2. He was "operating an illegal investment scheme, called a Ponzi scheme."
3. Dr. Zoller.
4. Kirt Nightingale.
5. He wanted to build estates and condominiums.

THE CAT WHO WENT UP THE CREEK
General Questions
1. He plans to investigate the "so-called" dark cloud that Lori Bamba feels hangs over the inn.
2. Polly "planned to tour museum villages on the East Coast in the company of her sister."
3. "The Legend of the Rubbish Heap."
4. There's "a circular staircase carved out of a single black walnut log [and] . . . some old furniture."

5. A bushy-tailed squirrel.
6. Dr. Abernethy.
7. Hannah Hawley.
8. The old furniture which, "according to the history of the place . . . were connected with the [Limburger] family tragedy."
9. Mr. Hackett.
10. He "borrowed a collection of Hans Christian Andersen's fairy tales."
11. She makes miniature furniture for dollhouses.
12. *The Pirates of Penzance.*
13. Hackett's oxfords and a green plastic box—his denture box.
14. The birthmark under his left ear.
15. "There's Always Something."
16. He is a photographer.
17. Martha, but everyone calls her Mattie.
18. 3FF.
19. An airport motel.
20. Nell Abernethy.
21. He borrows *Black Walnut* by Bob Chenoweth.
22. Koko managed to hide the pair of oxford shoes belonging to Hackett.
23. Nick Bamba whispered to Qwill that something was wrong with Yum Yum. Apparently, the Underhills phoned to say there was "a cat howling bloody murder."
24. The left one.
25. The Thompsons.
26. To the Black Forest, now known as the Black Forest Conservancy.
27. They believed the three veins ran under Black Creek.
28. Koko pushed off "Hannah's video of *Pirates* and Bruce's copy of *Black Walnut.*"
29. The first, a large moving van with a Wisconsin tag/the second, a tree that had fallen across the road.
30. The Piney Woods, Great Oaks, and Black Forest Conservancy.
31. To the Antique Village.
32. *The Beauty of Moose County.*
33. The video of *The Pirates of Penzance* and the Trollope novel Qwill is reading: "a Victorian novel about a scheming young woman who married for money, knowing that her bridegroom had not long to live."
34. Hannah suspects that Joe Thompson might be a phony. Her relatives say that fishing trollers don't go out this time of year. She thinks maybe the melody hummed by his wife is suggestive. Marge hummed Gilbert and Sullivan: *"Things are seldom what they seem. / Skim milk masquerades as cream."*
35. Qwill thought he was attending a meeting of the Moose County Community College, when in actuality it was a meeting of the Moustache Cup Collectors Club.

36. The shuttle that brought visitors from large airports to Moose County.
37. The truck belonged to Joe Thompson, and it had come and gone shortly after Qwill heard gunshots.
38. Marge Thompson, the woman in Cabin Two with Joe Thompson.
39. The cuckoo clock from the Limburger Mansion that was promised to Aubrey Scotten.
40. He has scattered them on the floor. Qwill picks them up but holds out another picture of the picnic. He wants to look in the daylight to see if there are any rough spots.
41. That "he's the guy who was trying to hire extras for a logging movie."
42. A forklift.
43. Tree stumps.
44. They knocked it off the bar onto the floor and broke it.

Chronological Order of Events
6, 7, 13, 14, 8, 4, 2, 1, 3, 5, 9, 10, 11, 12, 15, 16

Koko and Yum Yum
1. "Koko walked directly to a closed door. . . . Did he know it led to the turret?"
2. Koko.
3. They "had devised their own farewell: All the built-in drawers . . . were open—all twenty-three of them!"
4. Yum Yum.

Women in Qwill's Life
1. 7, 8, 1, 4, 2, 3, 5, 6
2. 4, 6, 1, 2, 3, 5, 8, 7

Qwill's Living Quarters
1. The staircase was "carved out of a single black walnut log."
2. Ground-up black walnut shells.
3. The living room.
4. True.
5. "Apparently no one knew it was there."

Dining Out
1. "Maple syrup and a dash of vinegar to cut the sweetness."
2. They make the crust "with vegetable oil in the new way" and "dice the meat up in the old way."
3. b, d, e, a, c, f

Crimes and Victims
1. "Presumably for his forty-thousand-dollar car and a trunkful of gold nuggets."
2. "Presumably because another gold prospector thought his illegal activity was being photographed."
3. Joe Thompson.

THE CAT WHO BROUGHT DOWN THE HOUSE
General Questions
1. Thelma Thackeray.
2. A storage warehouse.
3. Mark Twain.
4. True.
5. Homer Tibbitt.
6. Thelma's father.
7. Thackeray Snackery and Thelma's.
8. Thurston/veterinarian.
9. The Bambas.
10. Its circulation would drop by fifty percent.
11. "Derek Cuttlebrink's girlfriend and her two brothers in Chicago."
12. The Grist Mill/Derek Cuttlebrink.
13. Touchy-Feely Art.
14. Qwill and Arch's fifth-grade teacher.
15. Hixie Rice.
16. Lucinda Holmes.
17. Dr. Watson.
18. Noel Coward's.
19. 82 years old.
20. Mavis Adams.
21. Novels by William Makepeace Thackeray.
22. He decides to hang his new wall covering horizontally, not vertically.
23. Burgess Campbell.
24. "He fell to his death while hiking alone on the rim of the Black Creek Gorge."
25. Kit Kat Agenda.
26. Qwill tells Polly that he believes "the house she [Thelma] bought is the one . . . [Polly] inherited."
27. In the produce section of Toddle's Market.
28. Five/"There were six birds, but Chico passed away."
29. She says, "He invented the low-calorie potato chip."
30. Richard Thackeray.
31. Thelma Thackeray's assistant.
32. James Beard.
33. "California cuisine."

34. Thelma's Amazon parrots.
35. *Travels with a Donkey*.
36. Pat O'Dell.
37. They are kidnapped.
38. "Big square boxes, big enough to hold TV's."
39. There was a gunshot and "the loaded van took off in a hurry."
40. Dwight Somers.
41. "A retired police detective who worked for [Thelma] . . . at the dinner club. He was a security guard."
42. Esmeralda/Carlotta/Navarro.
43. *Richard Carvel*.
44. Richard/Dick Thackeray, her nephew.
45. *Poor Richard's Almanac*.
46. Polly.
47. "A pair of glazed porcelain parrots . . ."/Richard.
48. Richard.
49. Her collection of jewelry.
50. They were destroyed when Richard wrecked the van and it toppled over into the water.
51. Gambling and porn films.
52. Yes.
53. "THANKS, DUCKY, FOR EVERYTHING . . . written in invisible ink."

Chronological Order of Events
2, 6, 18, 12, 22, 16, 1, 8, 3, 10, 20, 17, 19, 21, 14, 4, 5, 15, 13, 9, 11, 7

Koko and Yum Yum
1. Yum Yum.
2. "Koko likes to know the hand that feeds him."
3. His tenth-grade teacher, Mrs. Fish-eye.
4. Koko.
5. He "sensed that something unacceptable had been added to his dish. He pushed Yum Yum aside and ate the contents of her plate."

Women in Qwill's Life
1. "He never . . . liked sexually aggressive women" and he considers her one.
2. Polly.

Qwill's Living Quarters
1. "Above and on both sides of the fireplace"
2. "A large sculptural wall accent"
3. Doug Bethune

Dining Out
1. Chef Wingo
2. a, bd, c, abcd
3. Junior Goodwinter/Rennie's Coffee Shop
4. Squunk water and cranberry juice
5. Thelma Thackeray/dining room at Boulder House

Crimes and Victims
1. "An unidentified male"/He was "shot to death at the wheel of a rented van."
2. According to the letter, "Dick . . . agreed to go hiking with [his father] . . . and would even buy some hiking boots. Yet, the newspaper clippings have Dick waiting for his father to come home from hiking, so they could go out to lunch."
3. By the conversation on the tape recording brought by Janice to Qwill.
4. We also learn that Richard killed his father by pushing him off the cliff.

CHARACTER IDENTIFICATION V
1. Ralph Abbey
2. Mavis Adams
3. Dr. Bruce Abernethy
4. The Bethunes
5. Dr. Teresa Bunker
6. John "Boze" Campbell
7. Delacamp
8. Robyn Exbridge
9. Ronald Frobnitz
10. Charles Rennie Mackintosh
11. Barry Morghan
12. Kirtwell "Kirt" Nightingale
13. Maggie Sprenkle
14. Jeffa Young
15. Mike Zander

CLUES, CLUES, CLUES V
1. *The Cat Who Brought Down the House*
2. *The Cat Who Saw Stars*
3. *The Cat Who Went Up the Creek*
4. *The Cat Who Smelled a Rat*
5. *The Cat Who Robbed a Bank*

PLACES, PLACES, PLACES V
1. Thelma's Film Club
2. Inglehart House
3. Grist Mill
4. Ittibittiwassee Estates
5. Northern Land Improvement
6. Absolutely Absurd Press, Inc.
7. Antique Village
8. Bushland Fisheries
9. Donex & Associates
10. Friendship Inn
11. Tin 'n' Stuff
12. Rennie's
13. Pet Plaza
14. Owen's Place
15. Pickax Curling Club

QWILL QUIZ V

1. To his moustache.
2. Christopher Smart.
3. "They're smiling."
4. "Ask Ms. Gramma."
5. Joe Buzzard.
6. True.
7. True.
8. 7 minutes after 11 P.M.
9. Arch Riker.
10. 7, 6, 2, 3, 1, 4, 5, 8

VICTIMS

1. Earl Lambreth
2. Joy Graham
3. Harley and Belle Fitch/Owen and Ernestine Bowen
4. Iris Cobb and her son, Dennis Hough
5. Earl and Eddie Trevelyan
6. Drs. Hal and Melinda Goodwinter
7. Thelma Thackeray and her nephew, Richard Thackeray
8. 3, 11, 9, 8, 12, 10, 4, 5, 6, 14, 1, 7, 15, 2, 13

SHORT & TALL TALES

A.

1. "The Little Old Man in the Woods"
2. "The True (?) History of Squunk Water"
3. "A Scary Experience on a Covered Bridge"
4. "Phineas Ford's Fabulous Collection"
5. "Matilda, a Family Heroine"
6. "How Pleasant Street Got Its Name"
7. "The Noble Sons of the Noose"
8. "The Dimsdale Jinx"
9. "The Curious Fate of the *Jenny Lee*"
10. "The Pork-and-Bean Incident at Boggy Bottom"
11. "A Cat Tale: Holy Terror and the Bishop"
12. "Tale of Two Tombstones"

B. g, h, n, m, l, k, i, j, b, a, d, e, f, c

THE CAT WHO . . . FOREIGN EDITIONS

1. *The Cat Who Saw Red, The Cat Who Played Brahms, The Cat Who Played Post Office,* and *The Cat Who Knew Shakespeare*
2. *The Cat Who Had 14 Tales*
3. Yom Yom
4. *The Cat Who Saw Red* (*Neko wa Koroshi o Kagitsukeru*)
5. *Japan*
6. Russia
7. b, c, a, e, f